YOU CAN'T USE THE G-WORD ANYMORE, MAW-MAW

Adam K. Armbrust

Adam K. Armbrust, Author

Dedicated to my grandparents, who never got the chance to read anything I wrote. And to my now-wife.

And to you. Please enjoy this novella about dating a goblin.

YOU CAN'T USE THE G-WORD ANYMORE, MAW-MAW

1

"Well, dearest, Auntie Liane says you've caught a new sweetums while off at Mage's College," said a withered, kindly-looking old lady, gazing upon the family reunion through glacier glasses.

Razan, a first-year initiate of Shiverfast Mage's College, nodded. "I wouldn't say caught. People don't really *'catch'* their partners these days. We... met in the library."

"Oh, putting all that book learnin' to good use," said a barren-headed old man sitting opposite Grandma.

"Yeah. We just started talking about, y'know, fiction. She writes some herself, y'know." Razan smiled softly. "There's a fascinating new genre that's all the rage in the cities: Alternate Systems. It's about worlds that operate without magic, or at least different types of magic. Long story, but together we've been collaborating on a short series about a world where vehicles are powered by a sort of internal combustion contraption rather than by enthralling a flame djinn to the driver's will."

The kindly old grandparents pretended to understand any of this, as was typical of grandparents doting upon their eldest grandchild.

"Well, we can't wait to meet her," said Lady Lise, of Rivergale. "I'm sure she's a charming young lass. And very smart, to be at Mage's College. I'd love to read these stories of yours."

"I'll see if I can at least get you a draft," Razan said.

"Wha-?" Grandma Lise asked.

"I said I'll get you a draft."

"Eh, there's a draft in here?" Lise cupped a hand to her ear, straining to hear.

The family ate a grand feast befitting an extended clan of landed gentry: Turkeypheasant, a local staple food; colossal catfish skewers from a far-off isle; and even potatoes, an expensive delicacy from a barely charted land beyond the sea.

Aunties and uncles were gossiping about their tannery or canneries further along the table. Grandma Lise and Sir Nasir of Rivergale, the family's aged matriarch and patriarch, sat in the place of honor. Razan's parents hosted the feast in their keep, Razan's childhood home. And of course, the young aspiring mage sat at the very end of the table in his SMC-branded robe, in the white and blue colors of the college.

It was his first feast not at the kid's table. The little vandals could be heard flinging potatoes around the foyer, requiring near-constant supervision from one aunt or another.

"Well, ever thought of bringing her home for the next Wintersgrip feast?" Grandpa Nasir asked, mouth full of potatoes.

"We were thinking I'd head to her place for the upcoming Summer dance." Razan twiddled his thumbs, a slight blush on his cheeks.

This elicited cocky jeers from the cousins. Razan waited for them to finish. He took a deep breath, then exhaled slowly.

"… and then we'll both come here for Wintersgrip."

The grandparents smiled. The parents meanwhile were looking for a place on the table to park dessert. Razan's mother always made a mean pudding.

"So, headed elsewhere for the summer?" Grandpa asked. "I'll miss fishin' with you, pardner. Where's she from? Around Shiverfast?"

"Well…"

"Oh?" Grandpa's eyes narrowed. "Is she from overseas?"

"What does she oversee?" asked gram-gram.

"Her family does have holdings in the city," Razan began, swallowed, then: "But they're from Fellmire."

All at once, Grandma's neck shot up straight. Her head swiveled over to look at Razan. Her hearing was fixed – miraculous!

"What *color* are people in Fellmire?" Grandma Lise asked pointedly.

◆ ◆ ◆

Ooh, boy, Razan thought. *Guess this would become a topic of conversation eventually.*

"You've, ah, been there, grandma," Razan said. "We passed through there on pilgrimage five years back."

In truth, she'd barely left the wagon after she'd insulted a kindly emerald-complected merchant by saying some word I didn't even understand the definition of, Razan recalled.

"Well, I don't know about that." Grandma Lise buried herself in a bowl of porridge.

Father made a point of clearing his throat with a grumble, a saving throw on his firstborn's behalf.

"So. One of them Goblins," Grandpa said with a mouth full of pudding.

He always had a habit of panic-eating.

"She…" Razan's cheeks flushed. "I believe she has an elfish grandfather somewhere in the family tree. But yes, she's a chlorophyllated individual."

"Goblin." Grandpa Nasir grumbled.

"Alright, drama!" one of the cousins said.

"Is she nice for a goblin?" Grandma Lise managed, reaching for the eggnog.

Razan took a bite out of a loaf of bread. "Yes, grandma. But, well, we don't really use that word anymore."

"She's a Green-skin?" Grandpa asked.

"We *definitely* don't use that one."

Mother clasped her hands. "Well, if everything goes well at the Fellmire summer dance, I cannot wait to meet Miss…"

"Domitia." Razan smiled warmly at the very thought. "And

she's quite excited to meet you, mom, and dad as well."

Grandmother Lise's head drooped. She could read the room; knew her vocabulary was antiquated but had no other framework by which to describe these revelations. Old habits, as they say, died hard.

"Is she nice, though? Miss Domitia?"

Grandpa Nasir ate his pudding ever faster, face unreadable.

"Is she?" Razan beamed. "Oh, she's amazing. She got a straight 'S' in every class, is president of the Women's Jousting Club, and has tutored me in Practical Potions 202—my worst class."

Mother and Father smiled warmly at the news. Even Grandpa seemed to grin slightly.

"-and she has a custom-made illumination spell that she uses to walk through the night market. It's a positively beautiful shade of yellow that hovers about two feet above eye level. And she made a miniature version she can summon in mass. Used it to decorate the ceiling in our apartm—"

Razan bit his tongue in a desperate attempt to derail himself. But it was too late! Color drained from his face.

"You live together?" Lise asked, her wrinkled jowls angled down in a frown.

"I... er, well," Razan stammered.

Father let out a sigh. He'd been obfuscating the obvious, hoping to ease the aged old lord and lady into modern Mage College dating dynamics. Mother gave Razan an encouraging smile – The Forge Lord only knows that she and Razan's father cohabitated through college, not that grandma and Grandpa needed to know that.

Awkward silence reigned. Still Razan stammered.

"Well, y'see. Rent is expensive in the city. It's... a pure matter of practicality," he said, puffing himself up.

2

Razan sat in a quiet sleeper car of an enchanted wagon. The cart buckled on its rails; the flame djinn must have been raging against its fetters that day. Outside, the distant steeples and bell towers of Shiverfast peeked out over the karst, illuminated against a starry night. The mage's college stood atop the largest hill.

His thoughts returned to the family reunion, and a conversation with his father on a veranda between meals.

"So, heading to Fellmire in a couple months?"

"Indeed. We already have the tickets." Razan nodded.

"Know where you're headed?"

"Her family has a clan burrow in the eastern reaches."

"Oh, that's away from the port. A full day's ride. Be careful out there."

Back in the enchanted wagon, Razan sighed. He was a grown adult by the standards of every kingdom and fief he could name, but his family still gushed and fretted over his safety. Some of it was warranted, being the firstborn heir, but he was almost surprised they hadn't sent one of the uncles out to Shiverfast to babysit him while he was at college.

The overnight wagon would arrive in Shiverfast's town square at dawn. From there, it was just a short jaunt up a hill to the college proper.

Already, the skies were brightening through the far windows, stirring sleeping passengers from slumber. The first sparse houses of the outer districts passed by in a blur, and by the time the tram drove through (well, over, on a magically imbued rail) the low-lying city wall, the landscape outside consisted of charming row houses along winding streets and up squat slopes.

Three days before the start of the next semester, he thought. Came back a little early. But Razan was sure he'd find ways to preoccupy himself.

The magi-tram lurched to a stop, and Razan was among the first ones out. The town's famous night market was winding down. A few enterprising stalls were still trying to hawk goods on clearance. With a rucksack containing his meager possessions in tow, Razan took a stroll.

Shiverfast was a city in near-perpetual winter. He'd packed a coat that went unused in his parents' rather temperate holdings. Now, he wore it over his school robes against a wintry chill.

Baubles strung up above tents bathed the night market in a warm glow, part of a still-developing field of illumination magic. All the big cities contracted summoners to place lights in public spaces in this day and age. It was the way of the future.

Most students wouldn't be coming into town for another day or so. He walked through the market alone....

... alone, aside from ownerless footsteps munching in the snow behind him. Razan turned, but no one was there.

"This doesn't work in the snow," he said, bemused. "I can see your boot prints."

An orphaned set of tracks rushed toward him, dancing around him. Then, he felt something cover his eyes – utterly failing to block his vision.

"Guess who?" came a cutesy sing-song voice.

"Huh. The light bending spell even works when your hands are actively covering my eyes. I can still see everything clear as day."

Razan felt the phantom hands leave his face.

"Clever, huh? If we weren't out here in the frigid hinterlands this would be quite an effective stealth spell. Someone's getting an SS+ grade in this semester's practical illusions."

With a wave of her hand, the illusion dissipated. Light

wrapped around a figure a head shorter than Razan, with sandy reddish-brown hair atop a light green scalp. Slender ears ended in narrow points angling away from the cutest button nose. Her eyes were large and saucer-like with pupils of the deepest and most alluring hazel. And she wore a wool overcoat, the better to protect her sensitive constitution from the cold.

"Have fun with my future in-laws?" Domitia teased. "I presume you've told them about me? I'd be devastated if you had a different girl at every port and swapped between us like some unknowing harem."

"They're... well, the family is... family," Razan said with a sigh.

All the stress and drama from the family reunion evaporated in an instant. Razan stepped forward, as did Domitia, and the pair embraced.

"Missed you," he said.

"Ah, so warm." She hugged him tighter. "Sorely tempted to follow you down there just for the sun. I can barely photosynthesize up here. My skin's going pallid."

Domitia's lovely green hue did seem a little lighter than typical here in the cold north.

"We'll be in the sun before long, my dear," Razan promised. "Just one last semester and we're off to Fellmire."

"Home again, home again." Domitia smiled, showing off her fetching little fangs in place of incisors.

"I can't wait to meet your family," Razan smiled back.

Domitia's fanged grin grew ever wider. "They're goanna eat you alive."

They shared a laugh, then made for the hill up to the college, fingers intertwined. Students at Shiverfast Mage's College came from all over and dated all the time; couples walking about were a common sight mid-semester. Domitia and Razan passed a she-orc/ half-elf couple who owned the local bakery, alongside a human-dwarf pairing they shared a class with last semester. A gob-couple waved to Domitia as they passed - gob-kind was rare in chilly Shiverfast.

◆ ◆ ◆

The pair waltzed together to their abode here in the frigid north: a simple apartment just off-campus. Razan had not been lying about how expensive rents were for aspiring mages slumming it far away from their family's holdings, but it was manageable when split in half. Being a spare dwelling from Domitia's family's real estate investments provided yet further discounts, ensuring the pair had spare cash after lodging, tuition, and food for ample dates.

They had a two-bedroom apartment for plausible deniability, should they ever need it. But alas, there was only one bed. The other room served as a work and hobby space for schoolwork and their mutual writing habit.

"Ah, dear, I've got a new idea for our next alternate system's rules," Domitia said. "What if all the lights in the sky are other worlds, and a sufficiently advanced enchanted tram could visit them all?"

"All the lights in the sky?"

"… were stars, yeah." Domitia nodded.

"Other stars, rather than tears in the aethereal plane." Razan stroked his chin. "I only fear that this may stretch credulity with the readers."

Domitia gave his shoulder a playful whack. "Oh, you. That's the whole point of the alternate systems genre. To explore new, impossible things!"

The pair retired to their bedroom.

"Watch this." Domitia smiled.

She clasped her hands together and whispered an incantation… and myriad constellations of pinprick-sized orange-yellow lights like miniature southern suns flooded the room. They naturally floated to the ceiling.

"Lemme close the blinds." Domitia did so, and they had a private night sky to gawk at even as the sun rapidly arose outside.

Razan looked up, admiring the spell his dear girlfriend had

been perfecting in his absence. Only, he noticed after a time that he was the only one watching the light show.

"As perceptive as a blind dire-rabbit," Domitia said.

"Do... do they have those in Fellmire?"

The pair gazed into each other's eyes, Domitia's hazel pupils aglow in the low light.

"I didn't shut the blinds or set up this mood lighting so we could gawk at the ceiling," she teased.

Domitia grabbed her beau by the hem of his robes and pushed him onto their plush double bed.

"Welcome home, Razan."

And they spent the rest of the morning (and afternoon, maybe even the next evening) doing things inappropriate for this story's rating.

Shiverfast Mages College commenced its next semester with little fanfare. Razan and Domitia awoke one day, donned the mage robes that served as their school uniform, and walked up the hill to begin another spate of classes.

They had more classes together than not. Neither would complain. Their schedules looked like this...

Razan's Classes:

POT2774 - Alchemy Essentials
HIS2092 – Nonhuman Folkways
SPL2111 – Combat Spellcasting
BIO2567 – On Mana Storing Organs
MSC1011 – Dungeons, Dragons, and 3 Credit Hours

Domitia's Classes:

POT2774 - Alchemy Essentials

HIS2411 - History of Human Magecraft
SPL2111 – Combat Spellcasting
BIO2567 – On Mana-Storing Organs
MAT3889 –Trigonometry

A busy schedule, but it would leave them graduating a semester or two early. It also meant they were by each other's side on any given day. Wherever they went, the pair was recognizable by their SMC robes in the school colors – white and blue, and of course their winter gear. Razan was hardly acclimatized to even light dusting snow, and Domitia was quite well-known for detesting the constantly dreary skies.

Razan helped Domitia with verbal history chapter readthroughs (by far her worst subject) while she hard-carried him through Potions class and tried (and largely failed) to prep him for additional math classes in the next two years.

◆ ◆ ◆

Crafting new spells or adapting existing ones was a common mode of study, if not one with its own track at SMC. The happy couple had a perfect opportunity to tinker in SPL2111.

Combat Spellcasting did not necessarily necessitate dueling, but it was an effective way of testing out new techniques and blocking mechanics. So, the pair borrowed the university gymnasium on the off hours for sparring practice.

"It's not like we can keep our spell tinkering a secret from each other in the apartment," Domitia said.

"Not much of an element of surprise," Razan admitted. "Still, instructions just say we need to customize one offensive projectile spell and one form of barrier…"

"Already beat ya to it," Domitia smiled toothily. "Ready?"

Razan held a catalyst up in one hand, pointing in Domitia's direction at an off angle, the better to reinforce his deflection barrier.

"Sure thing."

With a flick of her wrist, Domitia summoned forth a miniature sun in the middle of the gymnasium. The plasma ball advanced at a crawl at first... then accelerated exponentially. Razan scarcely had time to swish his wand in a deflective motion. The light ball screamed at him, hit the barrier, and dissipated in a whiff of ozone and a blinding glare.

Razan wound up on the floor, perfectly safe beyond a bit of singe around the hem of his robes.

"I am so, so sorry, Razan. Are you okay?" Domitia knelt over Razan, with a worried look on her face. "By Gorbgar's beard! All that, even with the school's limiters on this loaner catalyst."

"Would you get mad if I said this near-death experience kind of got me hot and bothered?"

Domitia shot her beau a piteous look.

"No flirting in the gymnasium, mister." Her frown turned into a sly grin. "Too much of that and we could get ourselves in trouble."

Razan chuckled.

"I mean it. It'd be awkward if someone on the faculty alumni list got disciplined for... uncouth activities in the gym."

"I'm sure."

Domitia helped Razan up.

"Someone's getting an SSS rank on the final exam," Razan managed, dusting himself off. "That thing was huge. Could've taken the city wall down."

"Hey, that was quite the barrier. Worth at least S rank." Domitia said. "If that fireball is impressive, the barrier that dispelled it where it stood has to be mighty as well."

Razan dusted himself off, a self-satisfied grin on his face. "I suppose so."

"Activating it with a waving gesture seems a little... inefficient. Requires a twitchy catalyst hand and perfect timing."

"Eh, it's flashier than a boring old barrier. And it dispels anything it hits."

"I suppose it did." Domitia let out a sigh. "Whew. Didn't expect to get winded during basic spell testing. Let's go get some grub."

3

It had not quite been love at first sight.

That came at a *slight* delay.

They met in the college library, as Razan had told his family. And they had started talking about their shared passion for alternate systems literature. She'd seemed nice. But then, she invited him to a jousting club tourney. Razan got one look at her atop one of the university's pride tourney horses, her squat stature bulked up in full plate armor and *whoooo, boy.* That got the old mana circuits flowing.

After that, he met up with her after the tourney was done. They got to talking again... and though it only felt like they'd spoken for an hour or so, they were both surprised to discover the sun peeking out over the tundra, a whole night passing in a flash.

That was a month into their first semester. Razan moved into Domitia's off-campus apartment just weeks later, and now they were approaching their first anniversary before midterms.

"Whatcha looking at?" Domitia angled her head off to her right.

"Nothing. Just reminiscing."

Razan smiled, which made Domitia smile back. Her ears twitched, a sign of bashfulness.

"You're bad at keeping secrets." Domitia giggled softly to herself.

"Oh, just get out there, dear. I'll tell you afterward," Razan said with a wink.

"Yeah, yeah. Keep your secrets." The young gob-kin woman giggled.

Domitia marched over to a tent holding both a horse stable and an armorer's table for her weekly practice.

Shiverfast Mages College owned a fair bit of property both in and out of the city. Classes were not far from the night market, but there was a wide field on the city outskirts for varsity sports. Horse stables and wide, flat jousting grounds sat tucked between where the urban landscape tapered off and where the cold-berry farms, which defined Shiverfast's meager agricultural output, began.

Thrice weekly, Domitia would head out for jousting practice. Every other week there was a proper tourney, and Razan never missed one.

Hours of prep time were needed to suit and saddle up. During this time, the early-autumn sun of Shiverfast drifted low along the horizon. But flame-djinn lanterns kept the course illuminated. Before long, Domitia appeared on horseback, her tight frame encased in shining armor emblazoned with sponsorships from local haberdasheries and highlighted in school colors.

It was a dirty stereotype that goblins were short and stout. Domitia was a solid five and a half heads tall in comparison to Razan's six-point-two heads, both of which were perfectly acceptable heights for any humanoid. Standing on her beau's toes, she was his equal in height. She could kiss his forehead if she stood on her tiptoes to make up the extra head on her decidedly average-height paramour.

Regardless, jousting armor looked good on the Fellmirian mage. She rode out on one of the college's rent-a-steeds - a brown-hued horse that was a little older than the other selections but reliably sturdy.

Most students rented out horses. Especially those who came from other cities. It was impractical to store one without a palatial manse and grazing grounds. But on the far side of the jousting course emerged a competitor who happened to own a small cavalry corps of horses.

"Hey, Noblessa!" yelled their fellow students. "Woo!"

Noblessa arrived on a white steed that matched her blonde twin tails. She wore lighter armor than Domitia. Much like her horse, it was a custom set emblazoned in the seal of her family of local barons.

"Did you know that Shiverfast jousting used to occur on the back of dire-cassowaries?" Another observer from the audience asked one of their companions. "Changes only happened in the last century or so as foreign horses were imported."

"Yeah, I'd love to see that. One match a year, at least."

Razan remained silent. He caught himself staring at Domitia again and then cheered for her as she rode up to take her place upon the list field to a quiet, respectable sea of clapping. Most watchers were there for Noblessa, but it was an exhibition match all in wholesome fun.

Marshalls played a horn over loudspeakers, though the effect was simulated on a newfangled daguerreotype these days rather than an actual instrument being tooted on the pitch. The joust began.

With lances raised, both combatants surged forward. Noblessa's horse was bulkier. But Domitia's steed proved more well-rounded.

There's no dodging during a joust. The pair presented a shield on their left shoulders. Here Domitia was also at a bit of a disadvantage, being left-handed and all. Still, the duelists met. There was a crash of shattering wood, then Domitia emerged on the far side of the tilt rail, broken lance in hand. Noblesse rode by the stands, lance merely nicked, and shield dented.

"Ouch." Domitia spun her arm around. "Got me right on the shoulder."

There was a murmur of excitement from the crowd.

"Three points to Domitia. One point to Noblessa," said an announcer.

Again, the duelists squared up. They charged, and…

Noblessa's lance shattered against Domitia's heater shield. Domitia's in turn broke only the tip of her lance.

"Two points for Domitia. Three points for Noblessa."

Again, the crowd cheered. While this was only an off-season varsity meet, the crowd of students remained energized.

Now Domitia was back on the size of the tilt where Razan could see her. Oh, by the hammer god, he was staring again. She seemed to notice as much and flashed a smile at the crowd.

Once more, the duelists charged. There was a crack of wood on metal, and...

Noblessa fell to the mulch. Domitia appeared on the other end, lance broken.

"Three points to Domitia. Zero points for Noblessa. Dismount."

"Good game, Noblessa!" said the gob-girl as she marched by and offered her hand.

"Good game," said the young noble heiress, and took her up on the offer.

With Noblessa back on her feet and confirmed to be uninjured by the field medics, the crowd cheered respectfully. Domitia did a victory lap, stopping by to give a salute to a certain someone in the crowd.

"Who wants a trophy?" she cried out, then threw her broken lance to the crowd.

Again, Razan caught himself staring.

◆ ◆ ◆

"Hey, how'd I do?" Domitia asked once practice wound down.

"Excellent as usual. Wanna go celebrate at Friar Destin's Dishes 'n Dungeon Dives?" Razan asked.

"Oh, I love their dire-duck sandwiches." Domitia licked her lips. "But you've got to spill the beans now. What's the big surprise you've got planned?"

"Well, you see, I know it's a few weeks away, but..." Razan dissipated a minor cloaking spell, revealing that he'd already placed a bouquet on the jousting tilt's stand railing.

Three ruby-red roses poked out from the top. And

surrounding them, a series of thorn-covered Fell peonies. Off-season on this continent, but, with prep time and a source from beyond the inland sea…

Domitia's hazel eyes went wide. "Oh, Razan. These are just like home."

She grabbed the bouquet and gently sniffed each flower. "Mmmm. There are guide pheromones in each peony. Subtle locational details. Not something you'd be able to recognize. But…"

"Was it to your liking?"

"They were plucked not far from the family burrow," she declared, eyes fluttering shut to savor the scent-memory. "Not bad at all. How did you…?"

Razan nodded, expecting the question. "I heard from your family; they told me where to source them."

"I knew it." She gazed at the flowers with a warm grin.

"Um, did I do good?"

"You did excellently." Domitia took his hand. "I do hope my family wasn't too overbearing."

"We communicated by letter. They seemed amenable."

The pair made small talk until they could reconvene at Friar Destin's Dishes and Dungeon Dives. Domitia looked out the window of the diner. A light sprinkling of snow had descended over the wintery town.

"At least they know you're coming. Wouldn't want to surprise them with a strange new boy."

Domitia stuck her tongue out. Of all 'unique' aspects of gob-anatomy, the tongue was the most human-like. A little squatter, the better for slurping up Fellmire berries. It was certainly a far cry from their sharper hide-piercing incisors, which poked out like cute little fangs when Domitia smiled. It was a sight Razan could gaze at all day.

"Guess not." Razan glanced away, feeling awkward.

"I wasn't kidding about them eating you alive," Domitia said. "At least, not my younger brothers. When I was their age, I was running around biting everything in sight."

Razan's smirk turned more neutral. "Really?"

"Pfft. No. By the time adult fangs come in, you're usually old enough to resist that urge. Usually." She took a chunk out of her meal, winter snow hare, a university staple. "Guess we ought to pack soon. It'll be finals, then we're out the door."

Too late to back out now. Razan gulped down diet sweet-mead. It was time to meet the parents – or the clan, rather. They didn't bite – Domitia promised!

4

Finals came and went, Domitia earning SSS rank in Trig, Combat Spellcasting, and Alchemy Essentials. A well-beyond-exceptional S in Mana Storing Organs would put her on track toward valedictorian. This track record was somewhat blemished by a paltry B in history – though perhaps it would be more accurate to say that Razan had managed to hard-carry her through to a passable victory in that one.

For his part, Razan got an A in Dungeons, Dragons, and 3 Credit Hours (largely a freebie, and they seldom gave out prestige S-ranks for such basic coursework) and Nonhuman Folkways. His beautiful and instructive sparring partner helped him ace Combat Spellcasting with an S, while On Mana Storing Organs was a surprise dark horse natural subject matter for him, netting an SS. Alchemy Essentials meanwhile languished at a B-, and once again, perhaps Domitia deserved the credit hours there for dragging him over the finish line.

With the end of the semester came the start of their first official couples' vacation. They received their final grades, took a short walk to the port, and then were aboard a ship for Fellmire the next morning.

An entire minor in recent magical-technological innovations was available at the college. Razan would've gone for it, but the scheduling was inconsistent and awkward. Where in their grandparents' time the journey across the sprawling inland sea connecting Shiverfast, Fellmire, and a half-dozen other biomes ranging from frozen hinterland to tropical rainforest would have taken six months and come with a necessary bout of scurvy. Not so now, with the simple application of a spellbound flame djinn exposed to an alchemy-concocted water elemental, ships could fly across the sea on steam power. What was once six months one way now taking three days there and back.

Three days round trip to Fellmire (and thereabouts a day and a half for Rivergale) made journeys back home between semesters viable. This magi-technology also produced rapid cultural exchange, such that two people from opposite ends of the inland sea could have a chance encounter in a third corner. Simply put, it was the reason why Domitia and Razan ever had a chance to meet at all. It had turned their alma mater from a sleepy little monastic cloister for the magically endowed into a sprawling campus that anchored the entire town of Shiverfast.

◆ ◆ ◆

Domitia and Razan had their own private room deep in the interior of this steamship. It was a third-class ticket – they were still college students on a limited income, after all, and neither wanted to go back and beg the family (or the clan) for extra funds. But they had a modicum of privacy at least.

"Mmmm. Cafeteria has carnivore offerings." Domitia returned to the room, rack of skewered dire-rat in tow. "It's a local delicacy — you'll have to try it once we're home. This cafeteria food, eh, it's not quite authentic."

"Is that so?" Razan eyed the skewer. "Heck, I'll try anything once."

Dietary concerns were only one concern within interspecies relationships. They'd both packed some snacks just in case they needed to tide themselves over – snow hare in Domitia's case, the coveted cuisine of the potato in Razan's.

Relationships between any two humans were blase and bog standard. A mage from Shiverfast and a noble scion from

Rivergale would've scarcely been worth batting an eye at these days, regardless of contrasting cultures. But one dwarf-orc couple moves into the burgh and suddenly the gossip of every guild in the Hanse is all 'how does it work?' and 'will the offspring have beards?' This is to say that more gob-kin boarded the transport ship at various stops along the way, homeward bound, but vanishingly few gob-human couples, or gob-anything else.

Nevertheless, Razan accompanied Domitia up on deck for the twice-daily sunbathing supplements. It was how she received essential non-nitrogen-based nutrients – synthesized them right out of the sun. By the afternoon after they set sail and rapidly steamed onward toward warmer climes, her complexion had already deepened into a verdant emerald green.

"Ahhh, this is much better," said the SMC sophomore, dressed in loose-fitting school-color athletic wear.

Domitia closed her eyes as she lounged back in a chair.

"Yeah, having to burn mana on illumination magic thrice daily was a bit of a drag. I'm surprised I still had enough left over for Combat Spellcasting," Domitia said.

Mirrored glasses covered her eyes as she sunbathed. If Razan looked over, he could see himself reflected in full.

"How did your family get to be landowners around Shiverfast anyway? If – if you don't mind me asking?"

Razan lounged back in a chair beside her – though he didn't get a fraction of the benefits she did, the extra tan wouldn't hurt.

"Hmmm. Probably best to explain before you meet the entire clan." Domitia remained lounging back, pensive. "So, dad was something of the black dire-sheep of the family. He moved away to get distance from nosy internal politicking – no privacy in the burrow, right? Anyway, he takes Mom up to the frigid, dark north while she's pregnant with a full litter. That's how my full brothers and I wound up born on-campus; dad got a tenured job teaching gob-origin illumination magic, eventually made some lucky property investments, and bought some off-campus housing. So, if you're thankful for our discounted rent, be sure to say a prayer to him during the festival."

"A... a litter?"

Domitia's expression was unchanged, save for her lips which angled up into the slightest of smiles.

"Oh? They didn't mention this even once in Nonhuman Folkways, lover boy? Figured it would've come up in cross-species anthropology the previous semester at least. A birth with five bouncing bundles of joy is considered normal. If we get a little sloppy you could be providing for a family of up to nine by senior year. Might have to find a larger apartment..."

"I, uh..."

"Relax." Domitia reached over and playfully slapped her hand against his bicep. "I'm on herbs. Wouldn't do anything that would cut my jousting career short anyway. Also, we don't really eat solid foods until we're near our teens – run on photosynthesis only. Ought to save on food expenses."

Razan exhaled slowly. Crisis averted.

"Anyway..." Domitia, too, seemed eager to change the subject. "Dear departed dad would've passed as a human mage if he could've found the proper glamour for it. Once dad was no longer with us, Mom wasted no time in returning to Fellmire. One additional litter from Dad and another from her new marriage make for seven semi-feral preteen younger brothers. Family reunions are a raucous affair."

"I'm sure..."

Somehow those hectic family feasts back at the ancestral Rivergale keep didn't seem half as hectic as they could be.

"So, when we get to Fellmire," Razan began.

"We'll be picked up by my auntie – mom's littermate. She's prone to judge. Just act casual, yeah? Then we'll get a cart out to the burrow, go downstairs, meet Mom, my brothers, and the rest of the clan. And then..."

Domitia leaned forward, smiling slyly.

"... I complete my mission to seduce naïve magically-inclined undergrads and trick them into our hovel, where we cook and eat you to inherit your mana base."

"..."

"That's a joke." Domitia leaned back into her seat. "In case it wasn't clear. People say gob-humor is dark. I don't think I have a grasp on it. Been living up in the snow for too long. Still, if I'm going to be home for long, might want to get back in the groove of things."

The sun sunk behind the clouds, and gob-kin passengers got out of their chairs and ventured below decks; their daily allotment of sun acquired.

"Home." Domitia chuckled to herself. "Only been back here for family reunions. And yet…"

◆ ◆ ◆

The ship made three quick stops on its trip skirting the inland sea. One in Widetower, the administrative city, mostly to pick up documents and offload tuition payments. The next was in the Warmarshes. Once a wild and untamed marsh (hence the name) was used as orc breeding grounds for their egg clutches. Human settlers cleared out the marshes some six generations ago to ensure the Freedom and Liberty of prospective future colonists. Colonists that never came, hence why the marshes remained wholly depopulated even into the contemporary age.

From there, the ship made one last stop in Centreport, an island in the inland sea, and major trading hub. Here was where most passengers either disembarked or boarded from. As little more than an extended-stay ferry, it parked in each location for no more than an hour or two. Crews worked hastily, ushering along passengers and cargo like a well-ordered machine.

For the Centreport to Fellmire trip, half the passengers were gob or gob-adjacent. The ferry would continue onward after Fellmire, up the coast to the north and east until eventually circling all the way back around to Shiverfast. In fact, it would be how they got back for their return trip for the next semester. But for now, the arid sand and jagged rocks of Fellmire awaited…

Fellmire was both a desert and a mire – hence the name. Water seeped out of natural springs in the ground but seldom fell from the sky, resulting in many streams and rivers but also scorching cloudless skies.

"You've been here before?" Domitia asked.

Razan nodded. "Once before. On a cruise. Barely left Port Fellmire."

"Eh, tourists seldom do. C'mon, this is hardly my first family get-together. Auntie should be waiting for us right outside customs."

Auntie was, in fact, waiting for them right outside customs. Razan could certainly see the family resemblance; she looked like Domitia if she were thirty years older and if certain features had zigged instead of zagged. A nose and brow had a slightly less well-defined slope to them. One assumed Domitia's mother looked somewhere between the two.

Regardless, Domitia hugged her aunt. They hadn't met in at least six years.

"Ay, you haven't been photosynthesizing dear. Your skin's going to turn blanched."

Domitia cringed as Auntie pinched her cheeks.

"The college doesn't get a lot of – ouch – sun!" she protested.

"I'm serious. You should summon a UV orb at least twice a day. You already are? Then four times a day! We don't want your skin to wither and look like some kind of hu– hi! You must be Razan, yes? She's written so much about you in her letters to the burrow. Got a thing for armor, eh?"

There was little time for Razan to react to that. His cheeks flushed, but before Domitia's aunt could inflict some withering criticism or another, a blaring horn from an enchanted carriage interrupted her. It was the two-minute warning that the carriage was about to leave. Steam rose from the front car as the fettered flame djinn was quite angry.

"Oh, but enough about that, let's get you to the old hovel, dears."

◆ ◆ ◆

Enchanted carriages on this side of the inland sea were not so different from the trams Razan took to get from Rivergale to SMC. A little less headroom. The pair kept their luggage and effects down near their knees.

Auntie (for her name was unpronounceable by human tongues, though perhaps that was a lie she told as a joke) had not lived with or around Domitia when she was growing up in cold, far-off Shiverfast. But she had plenty of embarrassing childhood stories acquired secondhand. Domitia's cheeks blushed a very pretty shade of brown as Auntie regaled her beau with the time she'd hunted down and ate her first carnivorous kill.

They rode along a rail for a few hours, along the rocky outcroppings and low-lying pools of Fellmire. It was a beautiful country. Truly a land of contrasts.

Having disembarked just before noon, the sun hung low – towards Razan's home far to the west – by the time they neared a rockier, less-mire-y region atop a high plateau. The enchanted carriage stopped, being at the end of its line. The paltry few passengers remaining got out at a simple platform, and the tram continued backward towards the port, leagues in the distance.

Of course, Razan had zero clue where to go. Auntie and Domitia led the way, leaving Razan to manage the luggage. They walked through the arid landscape, the sun mercifully less harsh in the late-late afternoon. They traveled to the far corner of the plateau, where it gradually petered out into more desert-marsh. Razan found himself peering down a truly massive, layered pit.

There, sunken into the very rock, was a hole. And in that hole lived his girlfriend's extended family.

◆ ◆ ◆

"Welcome to the burrow!" Auntie explained as they stepped down a winding series of steps circling the pit. "Whole extended clan lives in here. Grew up with Domitia's mom and the rest of our litter. Most are still around. Of course, she went off with Grubnab for a time. But, why, here she is now!"

Indeed, Domitia's mother and a gaggle of various cousins, siblings, and clanmates milled about near the burrow entrance.

"Psst. Who is Grubnab again?" Razan asked before the gob-tide was upon them.

"Dad," she said. "Went by 'Professor Bob' in Shiverfast. Don't worry about it, sweetie, you're doing great."

Suddenly, Razan found a scurrying flock of knee-high creatures with sharp but miniature teeth gnawing at his ankles. The bitey beasts nibbled at him intently, though their bite force was a little lacking, the only thing that saved the poor mage's shins.

"Ah, must be the litter from the new guy," Domitia said.

"You should say hi to your new stepfather, Domitia," came a voice from someone who could just be Domitia if she were twenty years older. "Reknarb is a kindly gob of high standing. And he respects the old ways unlike some."

Domitia let out a low grumble, drowned out by the din of several dozen extended family members. Auntie came to herd the newborns away from Razan's vulnerable feet.

"Say, Domitia," Auntie began. "What about your brothers? We were so hoping to get all the litters in one place."

"Well? Grek is in school, but we seldom have classes together. Drek is in the merchant marine and stops by once every six months. Oh, and Grob and Drob ran off to join some bandit clan out in the tundra."

"Aya, aya," Domitia's mother said. "It's because they go away from home and lose track of the old ways. I should have brought you all back to the burrow just as soon as your father passed."

Domitia's frown sunk even deeper. Meanwhile, Razan had taken to cavorting with another litter (of Domitia's full brothers, albeit a younger cohort) that were thereabouts three heads shorter than the aspirant mage.

"Heheh. Looks like you're going to last longer than the last guy," said one.

"Hohoho. Not like the last guy. He got scared and ran mid-reunion."

"W-what last guy?"

Domitia draped her arm around Razan's. She let out a frustrated tsk.

"Never mind all that. Let's go get your luggage sorted out."

The couple traveled down, winding along the outside of the massive pit that marked Domitia's family burrow.

"Did I do anything wrong?" Razan asked.

She kissed his forearm. "Nothing of the sort. Just... ah, this was a lot right out of the gate. It has me off-balance. Keep doing what you're doing, dear, and just find a way to get me some fresh air if it looks like I'm about to explode."

5

Gob-kin clan burrows were great pits descending ever downward in a circular fashion. Divots and carve-outs along the walls provided interior 'rooms' for living quarters. But the winding, screw-shaped path allowed for the entire pit to receive easy and constant access to the bright Fellmire sun during peak midday hours.

Receiving a healthy dose of sunlight was important in gob-kin culture. It fulfilled the important and biologically essential rite of 'catching some rays' by which they got nutrients from photosynthesis.

At the bottom of the burrow was a pool of water, a natural wellspring. The entire pit had been a big ol' sinkhole that used to flood up to the brim in ancient times, just another boggy bit of the mire. As the ancient floodwaters receded, a clan of ancient gob-kin had settled in – Domitia's ancestors.

Cut to the modern day, Domitia's clan had expanded the burrow, adapted the hole for electric lighting, and filled it with modern amenities and comforts. The bed was extra tall—Auntie claimed they'd gotten a big one to accommodate Razan's lanky and awkward human stature.

◆ ◆ ◆

A stifling hot afternoon turned into a cooler early evening. Shadows grew long as the sun angled ever so slightly towards the lip of the pit. Domitia and Razan were set up in their room near the bottom of the pit. The bed was wider and more plush than the one they had at home. The pair sat in this room, tired from their journey, which had lasted multiple days.

"So, is this your childhood room? Or what?"

Domitia shook her head. "I've been to the burrow maybe a dozen times. The longest period was for a month between primary school semesters. They set me up in various parts of the burrow. I have no attachment to this room. Or any room."

It was a while before Domitia spoke again.

"Ah, it's always mother putting me up for these festivals." Domitia kicked her feet. "If she hadn't moved back, and if the college weren't so dang frigid year-round, I'd probably…"

"I… kind of like this place," Razan admitted. "It's homey."

"You don't have to flatter my family, dear. There's no need to ask anyone for permission to date me or anything."

"It's not that." Razan felt a blush coming on. "I just find this place, this dwelling, well, fascinating…"

"Glad to know you find my ancestral old country hovel interesting in an anthropological sense."

Domitia rested her head against Razan's shoulder and just sat there.

"Thanks," she said softly after a time. "For being here. It's never really been home. Mom was on the boat as soon as we'd finished dad's cremation. It was a small miracle that I was even able to go to college. Only because I'd registered early and had a legacy admission. And she hasn't stopped going on about 'oooh, the old country's traditions' since she got back. Gets on my nerves."

Razan wrapped his arm around her.

"You, uh, don't want to take part in this festival?" he asked.

"Oh? What? It's not that." Domitia's brow wrinkled. "I'll do it. It's fun. I just… don't have any nostalgic attachment to it is all."

"I hate to ruin the mood, but, uh, who was the previous guy?"

"Hmmm? Oh, Sven?" Domitia snuggled closer. "Dated a dwarven-kin between high school and college. He was short, so the kiddos were more effective at gnawing at his ankles and other weak points. So, he bailed before the festival. You've already lasted longer when meeting my insane family. Congratulations."

From outside in the pit, a great foghorn-sounding BURRRRRR wafted up from below.

"Sounds like the cue." Domitia rose from the bed. "Feel free to come out once the moon's up. Might be entertaining at least."

◆ ◆ ◆

Within an hour of Domitia's summons, Razan heard rustling about in the water deep in the pit. The sun had dipped below the horizon, and immediately a full moon had bathed the area outside this cave with a beautiful, pale bluish hue.

Razan shuffled about. *Hmmm. Moon is out. Perhaps...*

He took tentative steps outside.

The exterior walkway wound gently down into a natural wellspring, waters at thereabouts ankle height. A lone figure swayed about in the shallows, disguised by the glare of the moon reflected perfectly on the mirrorlike pool.

It was a quick and quiet route down to the pool, the water supply for the entire hovel. Razan walked until the water lapped up at his feet.

There, dancing about up to her ankles, was Domitia. She'd swapped her mage college-brand outfit out for some silky whitish robes that notably avoided her shoulders and midriff. The robes came with a sash and headdress that Domitia held in her hands and swung around. And it all had just the right white-hued sheen to reflect the full moonlight.

Domitia's eyes remained shut as she swayed about, then opened her eyes just as she turned towards Razan.

"Hey, Auntie Yor'mgltchr, the water should be the perfect height for the midnight – yo!" Domitia nearly stumbled mid-sway, expecting someone else. "Uh, Razan, honey... how do I look?"

Razan gave no response, gazing intently and eyes wide, which was all the answer his gob-gf needed.

Another blush crept up on Domitia's cheeks.

"Like… like what you see?" she asked, glancing away.

This time, Razan managed to nod.

Domitia smiled. "You'll be in for a treat come midnight. I've got to perform a moonlight dance in honor of Gobnorgernackep, god of hammers and patron deity of gob-kin."

"I see…"

"Yes, you do. You haven't looked away since laying eyes on me."

Whoops. Razan broke eye contact, then suddenly found himself too bashful to look at Domitia again.

"So, this dance?" Razan took a step forward.

"Wait!" Domitia stopped him. "Uh, you might want to think twice about that. This dance has… fertility ritual elements. It's said that any man who takes part in the summer moon dance will be primed to, ah, begat new offspring. Blessed with a full litter and everything."

Razan took a step back, water lapping at the sole of his boot. "Oh."

"It's supposedly super potent too. Overrides herbs. I mean, it's just a traditional gob-folk belief. I doubt it's true."

"Yeah, probably not." Razan took two more steps back.

"Just… might want to watch from the shore, lover boy." Domitia swayed around again. "Told mom and Auntie that your family had holdings in Rivergale, and they seem sold on the whole tall-man boyfriend thing. Think they're already planning the wedding. Might let you come back and do the dance for the honeymoon though."

"I, uh, really?" Razan felt his cheeks turn red.

"That's… that's a joke, lover boy." Domitia laughed, still dancing under the moonlight.

6

"**A**h. Despite having the whole summer vacation free, I'm now even more exhausted."

Domitia rested against Razan's shoulder on the boat heading back around the inland sea.

"It'll still be a week or so until the next semester," Razan said, also quite winded.

The remainder of their vacation to Fellmire had been eventful, with great gob-feasts in a room that spiraled around the family pit. It was quite unlike the great halls that marked Razan's family reunions. If you wanted to talk to someone other than the immediate neighbor to your left or right, you had to get up and spiral along the winding rock-carved table. Razan was bitten at least thrice during the week, but Domitia managed to escort him through the reunion with his shins intact.

They were back in a private berth for a journey of several days. The ferry would be taking off soon, rapidly moving north along the western shore as they sailed into colder climes. But Domitia had received a nice dose of sun, her skin blessed with a healthy gleam that would last for an entire year before she'd need another tropical top-up.

"Ah, well, they seem to be happy with you," Domitia said with a sigh. "Maybe because you're rich and come from a family of lords and ladies."

While the get-together was a more raucous affair than Razan

was used to, he kind of liked it. He wouldn't mind trying an Anthropology class in a future semester to better understand gob-culture. It would certainly minimize any future culture shocks should the two families ever meet.

Outside, there was a whirling of magitech as the ferry pushed off from the Fellmire port. The boat rocked slightly, and they were away, back to college.

"Just glad we have some time to ourselves before classes start," Domitia added after a time.

◆ ◆ ◆

The ferry traveled north to Coolheath, where the scenery grew more alpine and temperate. This leg of the journey was quiet with only a handful of incoming freshmen boarding at the 'Heath for transport to Shiverfast. The only other stop of note was in Freezeport, an even chillier locale than the college town.

Broken glacier-bergs wafted about in the water here and there. The port was only viable here in the summer, fields of ice venturing out far onto the open water once things got chillier. Only three passengers disembarked at this lonely outpost, and only one visitor boarded. Within the hour, the ferry continued towards the (relatively) temperate taiga of Shiverfast.

With the journey back to college cold and chilly, the pair spent the trip below decks, mostly. They had plenty of time to hash out the inner workings of their next joint alternative systems project, among other things.

"Ah, I had all sorts of books back in intermediate mage's school. Think Mom took them to the burrow when she moved. If only I'd remembered, I could have brought a few back with me. There's sure to be some inspiration there."

The pair lounged about in their bunk after one of many distractions from their world-building extravaganza.

"I may have seen one." Razan had an arm draped around Domitia's shoulder. "Spied it in one of your book-alcoves."

"Wait. Which one was this?" Domitia stared at Razan, her lips tilted in a just-off-neutral frown.

Razan thought back and tried to remember the synopsis:

"Brave burrow-chieftainess Vahnessa bows to no man," Razan began.

The green drained from Domitia's cheeks. "Oh no..."

"... that is, until the fair-haired and handsome heir to the Duke Chadblade catches her eye..."

"By Gobnorgernackep, you didn't bring it here, did you? No more, no more! Say nothing else, before people hear!"

Razan started laughing as he spoke. "... will brave Vahnessa chafe in rebellion at her attempted domestication at the hands of her human lover? Or will – pfff – or will... heh, will she learn to love the restricted bodices and formal court banquets of her rival kingdom?"

"How do you memorize all this!?" Domitia buried her blushing face into their pillows.

"... wait, there was one more line:"

"No there wasn't!"

"One thing is certain." Razan cleared his throat to avoid breaking out into a laughing fit. "Those restricted bodices are sure to be ripped by the time the hunky scion of Duke Chadblade is done with them..."

"Oh noooo," Domitia groaned, half-crying, half-laughing. "I haven't read that in years. I'd hoped it had been lost, fallen overboard on a transport ship or something."

"We can go back and get it if you want," Razan said, chuckling.

"Not necessary." Domitia exhaled. "It's a pretty good book though..."

"I'm sure."

"I'm never living this one down, am I?" Domitia squealed.

"Probably not."

◆ ◆ ◆

Their ferry returned to the Shiverfast docks, completing its roundabout route of the inland sea.

Domitia and Razan waited below decks for the ship to dock and the all clear to disembark. There wasn't much of a reason to head up to the deck aside from watching the city come into view. They could do that from their window!

An announcer declared that the passengers were clear to go. As the pair got packed and ready to go, they couldn't help but overhear some loud rally on the piers. Only once they were on the top decks could they make out anything.

"New jobs! Low prices and high wages for all true Shiverfastians!"

A banner in Shiverfast blue sat over a makeshift rally ground.

"Ah, must be the Barony elections," Domitia said. "They start earlier every year."

There was a considerable queue to disembark. During this long wait, the rally's tone shifted.

"The streets these days, sure are a little green these days," said a rally hype man. "Hey, it's like I don't even recognize the old neighborhood no more!"

The rally continued. The passenger manifest of the ferry heavily tended gob-kin, though most didn't seem to be paying attention.

In time, the rally's main event arrived: some baron from the outer frost fields. Razan never even bothered to learn his name up until now. He was but one member of an entire barony governing council.

Every five years or so the Baronry got together to rally in mocking approximation of the combat and maneuvers of an older era. In this way, they jockeyed for power and influence for the next half-decade's Northwestern Baronry Parliament. Shows of support via rally were more polite than the old brawls and army-raising of centuries past. Or at least they usually were.

"Hello, Shiverfast. What a rotten dung heap of a city. Nothing like the charms of the outer snow fields. That's where men are men and true – human – grit can be found."

The crowd, mostly locals, cheered.

"The foreigners. The goblin – oh, we can't say that word? I'm going to say it anyway. The filthy goblins and orcs and knife-ears come here, and they steal all our jobs. Just a bunch of lazy bums who take all the alms right out of the church's charity baskets. Why, last fortnight a woman came to me, said she'd owned a winterroot plantation for four generations. At least four. Maybe five. But she said – now she said, 'sir, this farm has been a proud Shiverfastian institution. But my son, he runs off with one of the indentured servants to 'free' her, now suddenly, my grandchildren are green!"

"I said, 'We've got to put a stop to it. I alone will stop it, should you declare for me in the upcoming Barony elections. This tide is turning our bloodlines green, folks. But it won't for long."

Again, the crowd hooted and hollered.

"It won't for long," the baron repeated.

Mercifully, the ferry disembarked on a pier one over from the baron's rally. The noise of the crowd and the oration of the various speakers faded into the background, swiftly forgotten. They were just two law-abiding students in town for college. One of whom had a good generation's worth of roots in the community. The mage's college was a Shiverfast institution, having put the town on the map. Surely nobody would ever do anything to hassle its alumni.

The pair disembarked without incident and found the quaint college town apartment waiting for them. All the trouble at the port wafted away, just obtuse political demagoguery that would never affect the pair. Immediately upon arriving in their apartment, the pair fell asleep, exhausted from an oh-so-eventful week.

The second half of the year would be their final semester as sophomores. Domitia's jousting club was in peak season in the fall, and she relished tryouts for the more high-stakes tourneys in the second half of her college career.

Course schedules went out, and...

Razan's Classes:

BIO3274 – Practical Bio Magic
CSS3116 – Spell-Computing Science Essentials
POT3555 – Potions 303
MGT3899 – Management (Advanced)
SPL3790 – Essentials of Spellcrafting

Domitia's Classes:

BIO3274 – Practical Bio Magic
CSS3116 – Spell-Computing Science Essentials
POT3555 – Potions 303
MGT3899 – Management (Advanced)
SPL3790 – Essentials of Spellcrafting

... which was to say, that they had identical class schedules. The pair would be spending most days with each other, minus when Domitia was off for jousting practice or tourneys in other cities. The pair grew closer still, feeling practically married as they cohabitated in their off-campus apartment and handled every class as a unit.

Razan, of course, attended every jousting practice and at-home tourney to cheer her on.

It was another long, grueling semester, but in the end, Razan and Domitia's grades were...

S and SS, respectively, for BIO3274.

SS and SSS for CS3116.

A respectable B and a stellar S for POT3555.

S and S rank for MGT3899.

And they both aced SPL3790 with an SSS each.

Together, the pair redoubled their efforts at the mage's college – both academically and on the jousting pitch…

7

"**W**ell, if it isn't the jolly green giant," Noblessa said, shaking her head all smugly, drill-tails swishing every which way.

"Oh? Well, I *am* taller than average for my family," Domitia said. "May the best woman win."

Domitia held out her hand with its green hue and dark nails. Only Noblessa swatted the hand away with a self-righteous scowl on her face.

"As if. Might want to pack your bags. New baronry council's likely to run your green-chasing boy toy out on a rail too."

"Noblessa, what the hell crawled in your mascara and died?" Domitia put her hand on her hips. "Where'd all this come from? We got along perfectly fine in Practical Bio Magic just last week. You and Razan were lab partners and everything."

"Hmmph. Well, when you're a *real* noble there are certain expectations. A certain caliber of people you're expected to associate with. And you...." Noblessa sized up her gob-kin opponent. "... Are lacking a little something."

The pair of once-friendly rivals hadn't been able to have their jousting matches for a while, with Noblessa off in Coolheath representing the college at a cross-sea tourney. But she'd come back... different. Cold, combative.

When Domitia didn't respond, Noblessa looked her up and down again.

"And by lacking a little something, I mean skin pigment."

"Just shut up and get mounted," Domitia said.

Before the jousting match could begin, Razan met with Domitia.

"Are you okay?" He asked.

"Why wouldn't I be?" Domitia crossed her arms and huffed. "Just be ready to take me back to Friar Destin's for a victory supp. Righteous fury gets my appetite going."

Razan chuckled. "Go kick her ass, honey."

"With pleasure."

This time of year, the sun remained out even during these late-night jousting practices. That was not to say that it was particularly warm. Razan and many others kept their coats on here in this chilly field.

Again, the announcers summoned forth Domitia and Noblessa. Like before, they took their positions. However, this time an invisible tension hung in the air. This was no friendly exhibition match.

The horses charged. Domitia broke her lance against Noblessa's chest plate. Noblessa's spear broke against Domitia's shoulder plate.

"Domitia two points. Noblessa, one point."

The pair retrieved new lances and prepared to go again. Once more, they charged.

Only, Domitia's lance went high at the last minute and wound up with a glancing blow to Noblessa's helmet that failed to break the lance. Noblessa's lance, though, slipped and shattered against Domitia's hefty leg armor and shattered.

"Domitia, no points. Noblessa struck out of bounds. Disqualified, match forfeit."

Noblessa swayed about in her saddle, clearly discombobulated from the blow to her helmet.

"Hey, Noblessa, are you okay?" Domitia urged her ride over to her opponents. She offered a hand to steady Noblessa.

"Don't touch me, greenskin!"

An audible gasp came out from the stands. All had heard this, acoustics carrying it out into the stands.

"Well excuse you," Domitia began.

Noblessa galloped off, forgoing the tourney ground's stables and no doubt heading for her family's own private horse pens.

Domitia dismounted and trudged over to the armorer's stall. She pulled on the straps of her armor.

"Someone get me out of this damn thing."

Razan left the stands to meet her in the armorer's tent. Other members of the club assisted her in shedding the heavy jousting armor revealing an athletic undershirt beneath.

"We've had, what, five classes together over the past two years. What gives?" Domitia frowned.

"Um, we've got a rep from the college. You can fill out a report," Razan said.

Domitia shrugged once her shoulders were free. "Can't hurt. Noblessa's rich – like, rich, rich. Probably be a while, if ever, before anything comes of it."

"Want to talk?" Razan asked.

"You and I'll talk over dire-duck sandwiches. Just… fetch me that rep, will you, dear?"

There were murmurs in the stand, Noblessa's outburst was the chief conversation piece. A mixed group, though everyone was unanimously on Domitia's side. The Shiverfast cold shoulder at least hadn't spread to the rest of campus.

8

J unior year awaited. A whole sensitivity training course was set up for oncoming freshmen regarding their green-hued neighbors. All the while, the taiga and tundra around Shiverfast grew more frigid still. Domitia's conjured her orbs of artificial sunlight with increasing frequency.

Once again, it was between semesters when the pair scheduled their second vacation of the year. The Wintersgrip festival beckoned in the south, and Razan would travel ahead to Riverdale, with Domitia catching up following one last all-hands-on-deck jousting tourney.

Meanwhile, though, the baronry rallies grew larger and more raucous. Razan made a point of accompanying Domitia whenever she went out to visit the night market. Nothing bad had happened yet. Still… the day of their next trip to visit Razan's family was fast approaching. The pair would have to separate for a time.

"Safe travels," Domitia said at the enchanted carriage station in the downtown city square.

"I'll be fine. It's a trip of barely a day," Razan responded. "You be careful up here all alone."

"I will." She smiled. "It's a simple jousting tourney, what could possibly go wrong?"

The enchanted carriage let out a whistling chime. It was time to depart.

"We'll be separated for all of three days. Go on, now." Domitia sealed it with a kiss.

Razan kissed back, then stepped on the tram. He found his seat, then waved out the window as Domitia – and Shiverfast as a whole, receded into the distance once more.

◆ ◆ ◆

It was the same route back through the taiga and tundra, over mountains, down into more temperate lowlands, and finally to the near-eternal summer of Rivergale.

Wintersgrip was ironic as festival names went, certainly in balmy, swampy Rivergale. But Razan's family had holdings there on a hill within view of a walled river city. Just a bit more than a day's tram ride, then an hour or two's horse-drawn cart up out of town, and he was home.

Father, mother, grandpa, and grandma were already there to greet him. This would be a smaller gathering than either the summer jamboree with Domitia's family, or with his previous family reunion before the school year started. It would be a quieter affair, with the greater family spread out across the realm such that they were.

"So, how's college going?" Father asked as they met in the keep's bailey.

"Lowest grade is a B, but the others..." Razan paused for effect.

"In potions, I assume?"

"Yes. But otherwise... all S-grades across the board!"

"Impressive!"

Razan nodded. "And it's all thanks to Domitia hard-carrying me through potions."

His father chuckled. "We can't wait to meet her. Is she...?"

"She'll be here in about three days." Razan smiled.

The pair walked. Then, as they neared the door to the noble ancestral keep, his father said.

"I've, uh, primed Maw-Maw, and Pop. Trying to keep them from saying anything that could be... *awkward.*"

"Thanks," Razan said, breathing deep.

He imagined getting into a righteous fury should any of his

stuffy family make any snide remarks. Razan's head was on a swivel, just waiting.

Of course, it was still days before Domitia would even arrive. He had time...

"Glad to see you again, pumpkin," said Grandma Lise. "Are you getting along well with that... Dominatria?"

"It's Domitia, Maw-Maw, and yes."

"And she's one of them goblins?" asked Grandpa Nasir.

"We uh, don't use that word. She belongs to a clan of gob-kin, or gob-kind. They share a common lineage with elves back in the Dawn Age. And no, they're unrelated to orcs – in fact, maybe don't mention orcs at all."

"Right. One of those," Grandpa said with a grumble.

"What does she like to eat, dear?"

"Oh, meats. Voles. Lots of fowl."

"Aye, well, we do have that," said Gramps.

"Oh, dear me. I was going to prepare spell-roasted potatoes." Grandma Lise's brow furrowed. "Would she like those?"

"I, ah, don't think she needs those." Razan shrugged. "Maybe she can eat them? I'll ask when she gets here. She should be able to consume our meat offerings, Maw-Maw."

"Good, good." Grandma Lise leaned back in her rocking chair. "Y'know, we haven't had any of these gob-types over for company in, oh, ever."

Razan clasped his hands together. "Just... please be nice. She's very sweet and she has problems with her own family. There are all sorts of problems going on in Shiverfast these days and I want the Wintersgrip festival to go well for her."

The grandparents smiled softly.

"There, there, dearie. I'm sure there's nothing I or Pop can do that will scare her off."

The Wintersgrip festival would arrive the day after Domitia came in on the enchanted carriage network. The remaining days were spent cleaning and preparing, as well as visiting with the grandparents and various other relatives.

On the afternoon of the second day, Razan and his parents

walked back to town to meet Domitia at the enchanted carriage station. They arrived early, which proved unnecessary as the carriage was late by two hours. So, they sat by the carriage station, as afternoon morphed into early evening.

Information transfer magi-tech had not caught up to overland or overwater transportation. Which is to say that Razan had no idea how the jousting tourney went, merely knew Domitia was meant to be on this scheduled train.

Hours after its scheduled arrival, there was the blare of a horn from the north and east. The enchanted carriage gradually rolled into town on the rail.

Shiverfast and Rivergale were on far opposite ends of the line. Most passengers boarded and disembarked at various stations between the two far points. Only one silhouette shuffled about in the pale lighting of the carriage interior.

The doors swung open, and out emerged Domitia. Same as always... aside from a honking big ice pack taped to her shoulder and a smaller bandage over her right eye.

◆ ◆ ◆

"By the Forge God, Domitia, are you okay?"

Razan rushed up to meet her, causing Domitia to wince when his hand grazed her shoulder.

"Aaah. It's still – still sore, honey," Domitia managed, wincing.

"What happened?"

"Just a particularly nasty shoulder blow from a lance." Domitia hunched over, fanged teeth gritted. "Still won, though. Knocked the other woman off her horse, she just got a shot in. Almost missed the carriage, though; would've still been in the school infirmary if the tram wasn't delayed more than an hour for unrelated reasons."

"Okay, don't freak out, dear, but Noblessa marched out for our end-of-season exhibition match on a dire-cassowary. Insisted on jousting 'in the true and proper Shiverfast way. The human way!'

This was the first anyone heard of it, but the judges upheld it."

"Why is she even still allowed to go up against you?" Razan scowled. "What about that case with the campus diversity and equity department?"

"I, uh, don't think there *is* a campus diversity and equity department anymore," Domitia said. "Some baron raised a stink about it only a week back. Look, point is those dire-cassowary things are like eight feet tall. Horses were never meant to joust them, and she gave me a shiner."

Razan rubbed her shoulder. "Are you okay? Physically? Otherwise?"

Domitia cracked a toothy smile. "Got back around and tied the game on the next round, at least. Oh, she was steaming."

"We'll have the town physician look at it," Razan said suddenly. "And your eye…"

"Just a little bruised around the eyebrow. It'll be back to normal by tomorrow."

Razan's parents awaited at the edge of the station, looking dire.

"Is everything okay?" his mother asked.

"Mom, Dad, this is Domitia."

Domitia bowed, as well as she could with a busted shoulder. She offered her good hand, which Razan's mother, then father, shook in turn.

"Sorry, ran into a little trouble at the end-of-year jousting tourney. But I made it in time."

"C'mon," Razan said, "Let's get you home."

Rather than walk an injured lady on the scenic but slow route out into the hills, Razan's family acquired a horse-drawn carriage to make the trip in half the time.

Razan, of course, helped his girlfriend out of the carriage, then aided her on her walk inside.

"Well, hello there, pumpkin," said Grandma Lise, only for

her eyes to go wide when she saw an injured gob-person being half-carried in with her good shoulder wrapped around their grandson's neck.

"Got clipped in a joust," she said. "So good to meet you after all this time. Imma... go change some bandages out but I should be okay for dinner! Can't wait to try Rivergale vole!"

"Well, that was not quite what I expected for a first impression." Domitia winced as Razan helped her set up a replacement bandage. "Kind of abbreviated. I'll have to have a proper conversation with your folks later."

"Ah, you could have sent a letter on the train explaining things, I could've come back."

Domitia shrugged. "Maybe. But I wanted to be here to meet your family."

Razan looked at her with a soft smile until she added:

"Hey, maybe you could concoct a healing potion with local ingredients? Submit it for extra credit."

With bandages changed to a lighter shoulder sling, the couple hung out in a quiet backroom for a few hours before it was time for a late supper.

◆ ◆ ◆

"What are we going to do?" Razan asked, pacing about in his room.

"About what?"

"Shiverfast. Noblessa. Y'know." Razan motioned to her sling.

"Well, dear, I had plenty of time to crunch the numbers on the train. If we handle it right and without any interruptions, I think we're on track to graduate a little early."

Razan's face lit up. "Really?"

"Yeah. Again, assuming no failed classes or sudden drops. It'll be busy, but we can have our diplomas and be out of there this time next year. I can sell the property; we can live somewhere warm. Maybe one of the islands along the ferry route? It'll be sunny. Close enough to both our families while far enough from mine that they won't come visiting all the time."

"Sure thing." Razan nodded.

The couple worked out the fine print of this early graduation plot. This lasted until one of the keep's many butlers politely knocked on the door.

"I hope I'm not disturbing anything too lovey-dovey," the butler said.

"You're not!" the pair said simultaneously.

Next time they'd have to leave the door open.

"Your grandparents have arrived, young master."

And so, Razan's grandparent's second first impression of Domitia involved the gob-kin eating from the meat selection one-handed while be-eyepatched like a pirate of the inland sea.

"So, Miss Domitia," said Grandma Lise. "You said you joust?"

"Yep." Domitia wolfed down a whole chicken leg.

"Wow. They didn't have that open to women when I was your age."

"So, dear," Razan said, changing the subject. "You won the jousting tournament?"

"Scuffed and bruised, but I won." Domitia smiled. "Certainly, miss your morale support cheering me on in the stands though."

Dinner wound on. The family's new gob-kin guest even tried the odd and exquisite potato, nutritionally unnecessary though it may have been for her.

"You seem… very nice," said Grandma Lise.

"Thank you, ma'am."

"And such an appetite." Lise chuckled. "Welcome to the family, dear."

Grandpa Nasir performed a quick grunt with a nod. That meant the guest had his seal of approval.

Desserts came and went. Afterward, the small family unit moved out to an exterior patio to digest amidst the steamy

Rivergale evening.

"Ahh, this place is nice," Domitia said, finally able to rotate her shoulder. "Like Fellmire, but without that arid dryness everywhere. A gal could get used to this."

"Miss Domitia. I've, ah, heard that Fellmirans can have... litters." Gram-gram leaned forward, peering in expectantly.

Razan inhaled. Better Fellmiran than the g-word, he supposed. It's more a region than a country (or an ethnicity) but at least it was polite.

"Oh? Yeah, up to nine," Domitia said nonchalantly.

"Why, that should make for quite a few great-grandkids to dote on," Grandma Lise said with a smile.

Razan choked on the air, face turning red.

"Too soon, too soon, grandma!"

◆ ◆ ◆

"Well, I think that went well," Domitia said weeks later.

The pair was back in the enchanted carriage heading back to the north. Domitia's jousting wounds had healed good as new. And she'd traded her SMC robes out for shorter, sporty outfits the better to beat the Rivergale heat.

"The festival itself always passes by in a blur," Razan said.

Domitia nodded. "I can see why it was so popular – prefer to be down here this time of year rather than up in Shiverfast."

In time the carriage took off. Razan waved out the window at his family – and especially his elderly grandparents. By the time Rivergale had receded into a distant blur in the south, the pair rested their heads against each other's shoulders, suddenly tired from their second weeklong vacation of the year.

"It'll be a busy Junior year," Domitia said after a time. "But if we can keep this pace, we should have a shorter senior year. Plenty of time for an extra-long vacation post-graduation."

"Suppose so." Razan closed his eyes and smiled.

"Soooo, got a year or more to plan that. For this coming

summer, you want to go to your family's place or mine?" Domitia asked, then nudged him on the shoulder. "Must say, I quite like your family, dear. Very... sane. Calm. Stable."

9

Shiverfast appeared unchanged from a distance. However, as the tram came to a stop in the central square, they discovered an entire wall of city hall draped with massive protest banners.

"Shiverfast is a city built by and for humans!" declared one placard.

"Know your place and show respect for real native Shiverfastians!" said another, with a caricature of some sort of orc being forcibly booted into the harbor displayed beside it.

"Ah, the same warm welcome," Domitia said glibly.

"Want to visit the night market?" Razan asked, hoping to distract her.

The lovely gob-kin lass had healed from her injuries—another advantage of the southerly sun on her naturally emerald complexion. The pair gathered their things and disembarked, hand in hand.

"Let's just go home. I'm tired."

With a nod, Razan walked Domitia home. When they got to the apartment, however, they found streetlights broken. And on the door, a great greenish splotch of paint emblazoned near the doorknob.

"Someone playing a practical joke on us?" Razan asked.

Domitia grimaced. "Worse. Maybe we should get another door..."

Still, the pair found that their door remained locked at least.

They let themselves inside and continued with their day.

Replacing the door went on the back burner with their expedited schedules. Soon the paint faded, and frost covered the doorknob a bit. Neither put much thought into it, and two semesters flew by in a flash.

◆ ◆ ◆

One final jousting match was all that remained of Domitia's jousting career. Duly, Razan noted that he'd been there for every practice of hers – save for that match where she'd gotten the black eye.

What would this final match hold? It was supposed to be purely ceremonial, just a going away party for the senior class. But the mood at these practices had turned sour as of late.

Many of the regular audience members had graduated or moved out of town. Meanwhile, a new and raucous crowd had started attending. They didn't go to college as far as Razan knew. But they did make a point of harassing a varsity half-elf member of the club so hard she quit school entirely. They'd raucously cheer for nobles and dire-cassowary-mounted duelists, even if they were the college's opponents.

Domitia rode out and was immediately struck by a winter cabbage from a particularly rowdy fan. When Razan rose from his seat and walked over to confront the hooligan, he found himself shoulder-checked by a particularly burly man in a wide-brimmed straw hat.

"Pardon me," said the mountain of a man. "Blood traitor."

"What was that?" Razan said, only for the man to lumber off out of the stands.

When he went to look for the cabbage chucker, the seat was empty. Razan looked at Domitia with a shrug. Their heckler had slunk off without consequence.

◆ ◆ ◆

Domitia's final opponent for all her jousting career, barring a professional run, was to be against...

A hulking dire-cassowary stepped out onto the tilt and clucked.

"... Noblessa." Domitia scowled. "Should've known."

The crowd of hooligans more than outnumbered college students at this point. They cheered for their brave human champion who'd come to crush the dirty goblin.

The joust began.

Round after round, the pair traded blows. Domitia aimed high to offset the fact that her opponent was now atop a two-legged bird that towered over her steed. This same height difference also gave Noblessa a vastly superior angle of attack.

However, this same height advantage that made her a harder target likewise made Noblessa's steed an ill fit for the competition. Twice, she lost points for Failure to Present – her shield was not available to hit, so the round was invalid.

"Just swap out for a horse," Domitia yelled from the far side of the tilt. "Or at least get me one of these dire-chickens to ride."

The crowd was not at all sympathetic. Shouts of "of course, the gob wants special accommodations" bellowed from the crowd, alongside "she can only stand against a proper Shiverfastian noblewoman thanks to softball treatment from the refs," and "... probably only got into the college on a diversity track."

"Will you all shut up?" Razan pleaded into the stands and was largely ignored.

One final joust remained. Another failure to present would disqualify Noblessa and enrage the crowd. But another dead-on hit to Domitia's shield would grant Noblessa enough points to declare victory.

The horse and the dire-cassowary charged.

Domitia adapted, using her saddle as both a leg up and a brace all at once, she managed to meet Noblessa on equal footing and, with a lance-splintering blow, knocked Noblessa back atop her avian steed. Two legs meant the fowl-cavalry had nowhere near the balance to it, and it easily bucked its rider off.

There were cheers from the stands. The loudest was from Razan, naturally. Though about forty percent of the stands were still either actively cheering for Domitia or at least politely clapping. It just didn't come off that way when the Native Shiverfast brigade was so loud about it.

Noblessa got up off the ground and ran back to her startled dire-cassowary. She ran off in a huff.

"It was just an end-of-year exhibition match," Domitia said.

Most of the crowd didn't like this fair-and-square win. They started beating on the railing, threatening to tear the stands down. And from out of the din, a chant:

"Greenskins go home. Greenskins go home! Greenskins. Go. Home!"

Soon it was the only thing anyone was saying. Razan ran up onto the tilt.

"Let's get out of here," he said.

"First I've got to get the armor off, and this horse squared away," said Domitia.

The crowd only grew rowdier, practically bursting out of the stands.

Razan climbed up behind Domitia on her steed. "Just ride. We'll use the night market stables until morning. People have done it before."

"Ah, guess we'll be celebrating by ourselves," Domitia said, urging the horse forward. "I was so hoping the entire crew would want to come."

◆ ◆ ◆

The couple's celebration at Friar Destin's was a muted affair. Even Domitia's favored meal of fresh dire-duck failed to lighten the mood.

"Situation's been getting worse since we got back from Fellmire," the gob-girl said after a time.

"What do you want to do?" Razan asked.

Domitia ate a snow-beat fry. One of Shiverfast's local delicacies.

"I'm tired. Tired and there's not much we can do. Not while still aiming to graduate on an expedited schedule."

"After we graduate, let's get out of here," Razan said. "Just, anywhere."

"Anywhere warmer," Domitia corrected, eliciting a chuckle.

He fed her another dire-duck strip. She remained strapped into her jousting armor, causing her to appear puffed-up and taking up her entire side of the table.

"Right. Second, we get that diploma, we can plan what to do… elsewhere."

Sounds of a rally from the night market wafted through the diner as another customer walked in. Muffled sounds came off as angry and combative.

"Let's just go straight home after this," she said. "I'd rather spend time with you than out and about. Horse'll be fine in the market stables."

"If that's what you want." Razan nodded.

"It is." Domitia frowned. "Dire-duck is a little tough today. Man, it was just supposed to be one last exhibition match."

The pair ate in silence until they were ready to go. Domitia looped her arm through Razan's and the pair made off through a light snow. They shivered despite their heavy armor and winter coat, respectively.

"Ahem." Domitia got his attention. "How about the armor stays once we get home?"

"Huh?" Razan cocked his head.

"Mostly." Domitia grinned. Then, when Razan gave no response: "… not getting the hint, are you?"

"Do you mean?" Razan's cheeks flushed. "Oh."

"Yes, oh."

"Well, it's just out in the open and all."

"Oh, come on. Even the most smug and conceited nativist doesn't care if we blurt it out in public. Hey everyone, I'm going home to engage in perfectly natural stress relief with my human boyfriend."

Domitia said this at a louder pitch than typical for an evening stroll. Still, few turned their heads.

"See? Nobody cares." Domitia pulled him closer. "Come, dear. I've seen you staring at this getup for the past two years. Two. Years. You think I didn't notice you going gaga over the jousting gear the day we met?"

Razan looked down, flustered.

"And besides," she purred. "I'm tired of riding things. Now let's hurry it up."

The pair marched faster still through the light flurry of snow.

10

There were still a good two months of preparation and finals before the pair could call themselves proper mages.

Midway through finals week, Domitia was late arriving for her Spellcasting Trigonometry exam. She squeezed through just as the door to the exam room was about to close. She gave no excuse, aside from a glib, "So glad we're done with combat spellcasting," as she sat next to Razan.

Razan returned home a week after their last final.

"I have… our results," he announced.

"Oh? They came in early this year." Domitia giggled, then glanced about.

"Got something to say?" Razan asked.

"Nah." She shook her head. "You go first. I'll wait."

Cautiously, Razan opened the two envelopes that contained the final exam and course grades of their college careers. He compared them both and let out a big "hmmm."

"Did we pass?" Domitia asked, still squirming about from across their living room table.

"All S's," Razan mouthed silently.

"All of them?" Domitia raised an eyebrow. "Would've sworn I'd botched at least Spell-Trig. I'd buy it if you said I got a B there. C'mon, what are they really?"

Razan turned the papers to highlight their straight-S flush. Domitia held on to the lip of a chair for balance.

"Well, that'll do it," she said.

"Now we just have to walk up and get the diploma," Razan said.

"Guess so."

There was a moment's uncomfortable silence.

"What did you have to share?" Razan asked.

Domitia hummed.

"Okay." She took a deep breath, fiddling with her right pointer finger. "When we head off to our next place, wherever that may be. You, uh, want to look for someplace larger?"

"How large? Enough to require roommates?" Razan cocked his head.

"Definitely not," Domitia said. "We can afford a far larger place, once we sell Dad's old investments. Look, you may just want to search around for larger dwellings."

"Are we expecting guests?"

Razan thought Domitia was talking about hosting family.

"Expecting..." Domitia's cheeks turned a yellowish-green shade. She nodded.

"Oh." Razan looked down towards Domitia's feet, then back up. "Oh."

"Yes, oh."

"*Oh.*" Now color drained from Razan's cheeks as well.

"Okay, bandage ripped off." Domitia took a breath. "What're we going to do?"

Semesters-old lessons regarding nonhuman folkways and anatomy proved hard to recall. Razan kept looking down toward Domitia's midsection.

"How... how long do we have?"

Domitia grinned. "About a year. Thirteen months is the standard gestation period. Should be about a month along. Longer than humans are accustomed to, or so I've heard. But they'll be ready to run around as soon as they're out."

"How-how many are we talking here?"

"Nine."

Razan cleared his throat, then started choking on nothing. "Nine!?"

"Full set." Domitia winked.

"Whew." Razan exhaled, suddenly lightheaded. "Maybe I should sit down."

"Let's."

◆ ◆ ◆

The pair sat down.

Nine children. A year to plan. Razan felt as if he was light enough to ascend out of his body if not tied down.

"Razan, honey." Domitia put her hands on his. "Did you step into that ritual pool?"

"What? No, of course not."

At least not directly. Water had lapped at the soles of his boots. He didn't think that counted.

"Well, regardless, we're here now... a-and we still have some time to prepare and all. Should barely be showing for graduation, and we'll have plenty of time to mosey out of here before mobility is really impacted in the fourth trimester. You, ah, sure everything's okay, dear?"

"Yeah. Just... this is a lot," Razan said. His voice dropped. "Still, I'm kind of excited."

"Me too," Domitia said softly. "Just glad someone said it."

The pair giggled.

"Oh, and let's not tell our families just yet," Domitia said. "We'll let it be a surprise."

"Agreed." Razan nodded.

◆ ◆ ◆

Graduation came and went. The blue and whitish robes of Shiverfast Mages College certainly helped mask a growing baby bump.

As Razan walked up to accept his diploma, he barely noticed

the dean or the other professors. His mind was abuzz thinking of all the things the future would bring. Before he knew it, he was back in his seat, beside Domitia.

They marched outside, where an early evening blizzard was just winding down. They'd done it, they'd graduated.

"I've already forgotten the commencement speaker," Razan admitted.

"Eh, didn't miss much," said Domitia. "Let's just... have a waltz around the night market while we still can, huh?"

11

Thus began the hazy time after graduation and before the happy couple managed to move on to the next stage of their lives. Domitia used the remainder of this early trimester to investigate selling her father's various properties.

All around the night market, the once tranquil stalls and stores grew ever less accommodating. The pair stopped by a flower store looking for peonies only to find a sign waiting for them. "Humans only!"

Razan stood there with his hands crossed.

"Well," he managed. "We shopped there for years…"

He looked at Domitia.

"Come, dear. Let's go." Domitia frowned. "We'll just… go home."

The pair continued through the night market, garnering stares.

"Ah, I will miss this place," Domitia said sadly.

"Want to head back to Rivergale for the winter?" Razan asked.

"Ah, finally, somewhere warm." Domitia chuckled.

It may not be a permanent home, but it would be sunny and there certainly would be no shortage of work around the ol' ancestral family keep. As new mages, there were all manner of career options open to them. Court wizard, magic-based farm administration, magical mercenary if you were desperate.

As the pair walked, they encountered an altercation in a narrow alley. There was a store, mid-ransack by an angry mob.

Domitia hung back while Razan approached an onlooker.

"Excuse me," he said. "What's all this?"

"Dunno. Owner's some dirt-muncher."

"A what?"

"Owner's a dwarf," the onlooker said, louder, punctuating the epithet with spewed spit.

Razan gasped. That was a parent of an old classmate, he was quite certain.

"Where's the owner now?"

The onlooker shrugged. "Ran out of town on a rail if he knows what's good for 'em."

The crowd ignored Razan as he walked back out of the alley, despite his clear countenance as a more southerly disposition and the fact he was a learned mage.

"C'mon. We're heading home," he told Domitia.

"This has to cut into the mage college's recruiting and retention rates," Domitia said as the pair opened the emerald-tinted doorknob into their apartment.

"Hmm. Chilly. The heater's off." Domitia sniffed the air. "Could've sworn we left it on at least a little."

Their shared living room was dark. The pair stashed their effects on the kitchen counter. Then, Razan returned to the door to check the deadbolt while Domitia went to their room to ensure the window wasn't letting a draft in.

Razan couldn't help but notice a muddy boot print on their fine wooden flooring. It was a size too big to be Razan's. And they always took their winter boots off by the door.

The apartment had grown eerily quiet in their absence. The door to the bedroom was half-shut, with the room beyond unlit.

"Domitia?" Razan asked. "We didn't have some maintenance guys come in recently, did we?"

A door to an adjacent furnace-djinn room awaited, likewise ajar. They usually left both shut and locked when the djinn wasn't acting up. And yet, now it swung open, and a heavy-built figure in a farmer's getup lumbered out.

"You're not maintenance," Razan managed, dumbfounded.

Indeed, the figure's scowling face was familiar. He'd seen it before – back at that raucous jousting final. Razan had bumped into him amidst the stands. Now, the figure approached Razan quite rapidly, with intent.

"Hey, this is trespassing," Razan began.

The figure gave a massive shoulder check directly to Razan's jaw, cutting any objections short.

Razan recombobulated himself on the floor. That farmer-looking fellow leering over him.

"Down with one punch. That's right." The farmer spat at Razan. "Ain't know how to fight, city boy!"

Boy, boy. The farmer continued to call the graduate mage 'boy' in combination with various epithets.

"That's right, that's right!" bellowed the farmer, chest puffed up. "Get up and fight, city boy! Boy! Huh, boy. Coward won't even fight. You wouldn't stand a chance, boy."

"That's right!" The two farmers nodded along to each other's taunts.

The farmer's spittle flew about, forcing Razan to glance away.

"Won't even look at me. Too good to look me in the eye, boy?"

"Apologies, it's my first burglary," Razan said.

Instinctually, he looked at the bedroom door. There was Domitia, restrained by another barge-shaped farmer fellow. Their two assailants could be twins and were likely brothers.

"Hey, you let my boyfriend go." Domitia scowled before she was swiftly forced down to her knees by their second assailant.

"Found you shacking up with this greenskin," said the farmer. "One of them orcs. Used to gather around and take turns stabbing them with pitch forks, whole villages used to round 'em up and put 'em down. Now we give 'em fancy degrees."

"She's a-"

"Yeah, one of them goblins," said the other man.

"Greenskin," said the farmer, stern. "We ain't gotta be politically correct anymore."

"Actually, 'goblin' is a slur too," Razan said, still woozy.

This earned him a scowl from the farmer.

"Come here with your little green plaything to stroll about our city, childless cosmopolitans, walkin' your little dire-wolves and collecting sissy little dire-cats without a care in the world."

Razan looked back to Domitia. Her thick winter clothes mostly obscured her midsection. They didn't know. It was probably best that they didn't.

"You foreign college boys always look down on us hard-working native Shiverfastians," the farmer declared. "City boys, keeping the real Shiverfast down, you are! All these greenskins, come to steal all our farm work and keep us in poverty."

"Hehe, Lloyd, this one tried to kick me," said the second man.

"Hold her still, Karl!" The man gave Razan a swift kick to keep him down.

The farmer accosting Razan, 'Lloyd,' examined the walls of the couple's abode.

"Jousting?" Lloyd frowned and then pointed at Domitia accusatorily. "You're the one they let on the college team. Getting your jollies off from striking our proper human noblewomen, are you? Orcs shouldn't even be allowed in women's sports. Why, it ought to be a crime!"

"I'm not a-"

"College administrators let you in just so you could use your natural strength to overpower our proper human noblewoman. Yeah! Your kind only get into positions of power on diversity hires."

"Did Noblessa send you?" Razan asked, coughing up a bit of blood as he did so.

The look on Lloyd's face indicated that he'd never heard of any Noblessa. It told Razan what he needed to know.

"Native Shiverfast has kept our eye on the nonhuman element," Lloyd explained. "Kept that green paint on your door so we knew right where you were hiding when the time came, greenskin."

"I assumed as much," Domitia said.

Razan grimaced. They should've changed the knob. Probably wouldn't have avoided a confrontation like this forever but may've bought them just enough time to make for warmer climes, like they'd been planning.

"Answer me this, greenskin." Lloyd's enmity turned to Domitia, still on her knees. "How long have you been stinking up our city?"

"Would you believe I was born here?" Domitia said, then exhaled in a stressed sigh.

"Bah, city folk just let anyone in," grumbled Lloyd. "Going to send you back to your mud hut, greenskin. How do you like that? Hmmm." Lloyd ran up to grab Domitia by the chin. "Answer that, savage. Hurry up!"

"It's more of a pit," Domitia said all matter-of-factly.

Lloyd struck her against the cheek, leaving an off-yellowish welt.

"Don't you run your mouth unless I ask it, greenskin." Lloyd spat this last word out into her face.

"You stay away from her." Razan had finally managed to get to his feet, balancing on the kitchen counter.

"Or what, city boy?" Puffed up, Lloyd paced back toward Razan's position.

Domitia tried to get back to her own feet but gasped, then looked down at her stomach, her aching cheek forgotten.

"A kick," she mouthed, just managing to rub a protective hand over her belly.

Even their farmer assailant could put two and two together there.

"Oh-ho. Mage boy got the greenskin pregnant," Lloyd huffed. "Trying to replace us with a sea of green, you are! Fill the city with orc types out to mooch off our generous benefits."

Lloyd paced about as if he couldn't decide which victim to antagonize next.

"Yeah, I see all those goblin workers in the farm stables. They're out to steal our bountiful farmland, take it right out of the hands of hardworking Shiverfastians."

"No two sentences you've said since you barged in here have been remotely consistent." Razan rubbed his jaw. That shoulder check had nearly dislodged it.

Things were escalating fast. Razan glanced about, looking for a way to end this before the farmers finished whatever foul purpose they'd broken in for.

"Out to replace us – just like those barons said!" Lloyd had decided on which victim to terrorize next. He moved towards Domitia. "Protected by these feckless city folk. Bet you didn't expect us poor, beleaguered farming folk of the north to fight back."

Lloyd rushed up towards Domitia, preparing to deliver a mighty kick to her abdomen. Razan gritted his teeth. Finally, his hand grabbed an oblong stick they'd left on the kitchen counter some weeks ago. He pointed it at Lloyd and, with a flick of his wrist, fired off a customized magic missile spell – the exact kind he and Domitia had been working on for Combat Spellcasting.

Magic missile twisted about, a vortex twisting around the central 'bullet.' It hit Lloyd right as one foot was off the ground, ready to kick, and quickly swept him away. Lloyd spun about like he'd been caught in a whirlwind, eventually flying back into the heating closet, with the door swinging shut in his wake. He was the furnace-djinn's problem now.

Intimidated and not expecting to encounter magic when assaulting this mage's house, Karl looked to the furnace room door, then back to Razan in a dumbstruck stupor. Domitia took this time to rise to her feet, turn, and give Karl a big bite to the neck.

Karl screamed until Domitia relented, and then he crawled away reduced to a bubbling mess. He'd forgotten about his brother Lloyd, still in a heap in the flame djinn furnace room. Karl dived right out the bedroom window with a crash. A chill night wind came in.

"Are you okay!?" Razan ran up to Domitia.

The gob-kin wiped blood off her lips. "Bleh. Hate that taste. Ah, that was close, though. Good hit, honey."

The pair kissed.

The open window brought with it the sound of more breaking glass and raucous crowds from somewhere down the street.

"We should go," Razan said.

Domitia nodded. "Don't have to tell me twice."

They would have to sell her father's properties in absentia, assuming there were any properties left to sell after tonight.

The pair took only what they could carry, prioritizing their spell catalysts and their rolled-up diplomas, and took off into the night.

◆ ◆ ◆

"Wait, wait, we can't leave yet!" Domitia said.

They were at the tram station. The conductor was a friendly face who specifically held the tram back so that they and others could get a non-stop ride down to Rivergale.

Behind them, the city smoldered. Armed mobs set about looting nonhuman establishments and even the College of Nonhuman Studies on campus. Splayed on the side of the carriage station was a bit of graffiti: a crudely drawn horse with a big X through it, compared to a noble and detailed dire-cassowary. The bird-steed represented noble native Shiverfastian fauna, while the lowly horse was a dirty import. And below all this, in big blocky letters: *Uphold our noble pastime. Purge the foreign steeds.*

"They're gonna kill all the horses," Domitia said with a sympathetic pout. "'Cause they're not native, see? C'mon, we got to get to the stables at least."

Razan looked at the tram, then to his girlfriend.

"They can't wait that long," Razan said.

"We'll catch up." Domitia cracked a smile.

Razan had a flicker of understanding. "O-okay. Let's just hurry up."

The station attendant said he could delay the train five minutes before departing. The pair had no problem with this – they weren't aiming for the station.

◆ ◆ ◆

The off-campus jousting tilt was abandoned. Few visited without a match underway. In the recent unpleasantness, even the groundskeeper was missing.

"Okay, we get my steed, free the rest of the horses before someone comes to cull them and lead them southward." Domitia nodded. "Just follow me, dear."

The pair snuck through the tilt to the stables. As they advanced, they couldn't help but notice there was a light in the armorer's chamber.

"Hey, who's there?" Domitia asked, her voice hoarse from all their exertion.

"Oh!" There was a surprised figure within. There was a rustling of fabric and out poked the head of a refined noblewoman.

"Noblessa?" Razan scowled. "What're you doing out here at this hour?"

Out popped the face of a pointy-eared armorer. One of the elves from the jousting team. Noblessa tried to bat him back out of view, to no avail.

"*Hypocrite!*" Domitia pointed an accusatory finger.

"Just… take what you must and go," said Noblessa sheepishly. "I won't alert any of the mobs. For now."

Domitia dragged Razan into the stables in a huff. She found her prized steed while instructing Razan in how to open the stables up for the rest of the herd. With their task done, Razan climbed onto Domitia's horse, behind her of course, and the pair prepared to take off.

With a cry, Domitia urged the horses forward. They galloped out onto the tilt and were naturally herded southward.

"One of these days, they're going to come for the knife-ears too. And then I won't be here to help you!" Domitia said, staying behind to taunt Noblessa.

With a kick, Domitia and Razan galloped off to the south.

12

Domitia and Razan rode up to the tram, now steaming at a moderate clip along its southerly route. They pulled up beside it and, without losing momentum, Razan awkwardly dismounted. Domitia had an easier time of it and hardly needed help.

"Well, guess I won't be able to do that much longer," Domitia said, and giggled. "Going to have to learn to ride like a proper lady, protect my tummy, yeah?"

The horse broke off and continued to gallop free with the rest of the college's show horses amidst the chilly hinterlands. Domitia waved the steed off.

"He'll be fine," she said.

Certainly, the herd would have better chances out on the open plains than trapped in their stables. If the college had any objections – if there was a college left after all this – they could bill her. It's not like either of them would ever be back.

"Thanks for keeping the tram waiting as long as possible," Domitia said to the conductors.

They had no luggage; they only managed to take what they could carry in their robe pockets. But they were safe and heading towards Razan's family's house in Rivergale.

"Sure hope my brothers are okay," Domitia said, looking back at the smoldering bonfires to the north. "Most stick well clear of the city these days. Still, I worry, y'know?"

◆ ◆ ◆

The tram continued straight on until the climate warmed considerably.

The trip passed in relative silence. Razan stepped off the tram briefly at the quieter stops to send messages ahead by magi-gram. A full day passed on the rails, and they arrived at Rivergale hours before dawn.

The family was there to greet him at the station. Mom and dad but no cousins. Grandpa Nasir and Grandma Lise were notably not present.

"Ready to go?" Razan asked.

Domitia peeked out the car door briefly. "I'll be fine. I mean, I'm not showing yet. If we stay here for more than a few months though, I mean, we'll have to tell them eventually."

"Of course." Razan's heart started beating faster. "You've met most everyone here already. Let's just... cross that bridge when we come to it."

"Sure." Domitia took his hand and kissed it, and the pair stepped off the tram.

◆ ◆ ◆

A great deal of fussing ensured, particularly by Razan's mom.

"Oh me, oh my!" she said. "You're filthy. Whatever happened?"

"We haven't taken a shower in a few days, now." Razan grimaced as his mom fussed.

"Well, let's get you home. Come, do you have any luggage?"

The pair shook their heads. Domitia hung back a little, still dressed in their school color-branded coat for more northerly climes.

Razan's dad had acquired a more traditional horse-drawn carriage. The family piled in, and they traveled to the ancestral keep.

"So, where's Maw-Maw and Paw-Paw?" asked Razan.

"Out on a long-term camping trip to the southern marshes," said his father. "They'll be out of contact for a few weeks still."

Ah, that would make announcing their surprise to the entire family a bit difficult.

"Whatever is happening up there?" Razan's mother asked. "I'll say. Angry mobs, kicking my own son out of his college dorm? The nerve of those northerners."

For the good of everyone in the carriage, Razan did not dwell long on who the family supported during the barony elections. How many of the baronry's supporters had wound up forced out of Shiverfast, their shops burnt, homes ransacked…

They arrived at the keep in short order. Razan and Domitia freshened up, then didn't even remember going to sleep.

Days passed, safe in the keep. The baronry controlled this region along the inland sea as well. But the city and surrounding countryside of Rivergale was quiet, owing to the most stable economy or more diverse populous within town.

Razana and Domitia had a mini-suite in one of the keep's quieter towers. Good, as Domitia awoke daily sick to her stomach, a condition they managed to hide from the servants well enough.

On the third day of this, Domitia found herself laying back against a wall in the tower water closet.

"Full litter morning sickness." Domitia crumpled her face. "Bleh."

A knock on the suite's grand door interrupted the pair.

"Mom and dad have assigned a castellan to our suite," Razan explained. "Need me to go wave him off?"

But Domitia had already composed herself.

"Ah, let's just let him in."

With a nod, Razan went to the door.

"Good evening, young master," said the castellan. "An important message for your paramour."

"Um, Domitia." Razan sheepishly invited her to the door.

The castellan produced a letter from a coat pocket. He handed it to Domitia – reiterating it was for her eyes only. Letter in hand, Domitia opened the seal and read it.

"It's… my brothers," she said, expression neutral. "They made it out!"

Razan leaned over her shoulder. He'd never seen her full brothers, despite their mostly still living around the old college town.

"Sounds like they're headed back home." Domitia sighed. "Ah, we weren't born in Fellmire. Weird to call it home. Guess our stunt with the dire-horses caused someone to notice us, reported a gob-kind woman heading south."

"How'd they know you went to my family keep?" Razan asked.

Domitia grinned. "Just because I don't hang out with my brothers doesn't mean I haven't told them what I'm up to. We send each other letters. Well, everyone but Gorb; I still don't think he can read…"

◆ ◆ ◆

The days passed with the couple continuing to lie low, ignorant of the political situation of contemporary Rivergale. It was then, after a week or so holed up in the keep, that Domitia insisted they inform Razan's parents of upcoming additions to the family.

And so, Domitia stood before the parents of her boyfriend, Razan standing supportively beside her.

"Mister and Mrs…. Razan's parents," she began. "Your son and I, we've got an announcement…"

"Did he propose?" asked Razan's mom.

Domitia flushed emerald. "Ah, not yet." She looked at Razan. "Will that be a problem?"

"Let's do this together." Razan took her hand.

The pair took a deep breath and prepared to blurt it all out at once. They opened their mouths, and…

The great hall doors swung open.

"Mob in the bailey!" bellowed the castellan. "Angry mob in the bailey!"

"What, now!?" Domitia barked.

Razan's parents leaped out of their seats.

"Whatever for?" asked Razan's mom.

"They say we're smuggling gob-kin into the town by the hundreds through secret underground tunnels." The castellan punctuated this like a question.

"Impossible. The water table in Rivergale is far too high to even have tunnels," said the father.

Someone should've told the mob that. In the dead silence that followed, the room could hear shouts and raucous jeers from the keep bailey.

"Well, don't just stand there," barked Razan's mom. "Barricade the doors."

Domitia took two steps forward. "We'll sneak out the back door. Just distract them while we escape."

"We'll marshal the butlers and have them escort you to the port under full guard. I insist," said the mother.

"Don't worry," said Domitia, with a wink. "We have a secret weapon?"

"We do?" Razan asked.

"No snow." Domitia gestured down at her feet.

Razan's father escorted the pair to a back entrance out behind the guest tower.

"You all sure you'll be alright?"

The pair nodded. "We'll be on a ship outbound before anyone knows we're gone."

Domitia whispered an incantation until light wrapped around her. Soon there was no evidence of a recently-pregnant gob-kin woman standing there by the door at all.

"Stay safe," said the father.

Razan looked around. There was no telling when he'd be back

to his ancestral family keep, if ever.

"Ah, tell maw-maw and pop that I'm sorry we couldn't see each other while we were in town."

"Don't worry. I'll tell 'em."

Without warning, Razan's father embraced him.

"Congrats, by the way. Name one after pop."

Razan cocked his head. "Huh?"

The pair shared a look.

"You know what I mean."

"When the heck did you find that out?"

"There's a limited number of reasons why a young man of your age would call an all-hands-on-deck family meeting."

"Fair enough."

Sounds of commotion came from down the hall.

"Go, go!" His father pushed Razan out the door. "They should bug off once it's clear we don't have any underground tunnels."

With a nod, Razan began muttering his own invisibility spell. Soon he hid in perfect shadow courtesy of Domitia's customized invisibility spell – with no clue where his girlfriend had run off too.

"Psst. Over here." A voice with no source wafted out of the reeds.

The reeds rustled slightly, and Razan walked until he ran into an invisible figure.

"Hey, that's me. C'mon, hold hands so we don't get separated!"

The pair ran off, paralleling the road to the keep as they fled, perfectly invisible, towards the main port of Rivergale.

Along the way, they passed perilously close to a mob guarding the path out. To the couple's surprise, they found that at least one of every six members of the mob was gob-kin or an orc.

A rotund man wearing great golden garb stood on a soap box, addressing the crowd. Razan recognized the man as a local magi-carriage dealership owner.

"Yes, the nobles of this land hate the common people!" The speaker flung a gold-ring-encased hand around wildly, motioning to the keep. "They send all these goblins to take all the jobs. Yes, after them, peons! They'll never be a man of the people like me."

Over at the edge of camp, an orc and a goblin stood watch looking down the road to town.

"Back in my day, we snuck over the border from Fellmire the old-fashioned way!" said a gob-kin. "Only a single rucksack to our name!"

The orc nodded. "Now these nobles bring in gob-kin and give 'em nothing but handouts. I hope the boss cleans up all those foreigners in the apartments downtown. They're pushing rents up!"

Domitia and Razan snuck past the group out for their blood in total stealth. They took a moment to appreciate the fact that Rivergale's angry mobs were at least a coalition of concerned parties compared to the groups of homogenous Fellmire lynch mobs. How swell!

The occasional fern rustling was the only evidence that anyone was fleeing in the night. The pair made it well out of bounds of the family lands, when...

"Hey! Footprints in the mud. Over here!" came a distant shout.

"Well, that's not good," whispered Domitia.

"We could walk backwards then climb up a tree," Razan suggested.

"Don't bother. Just lead 'em through rough terrain. We'll be halfway to town before they get anywhere close."

The pair fled until they were in Rivergale proper. A mob had already ransacked the tram station. It wouldn't take them anywhere safe, anyway. They'd need to get to the port. They'd need to get a boat to Fellmire.

A precarious few blocks remained between them and the port district. Mobs had taken to trashing apartments and shops here, too. Though it seemed a bit more targeted than the random violence of Fellmire. Many carriage dealerships had been ransacked, for instance. Not because they'd been owned by 'greenskins' but more because they were competition to that gold ring-hawking mob leader, most likely.

The invisibility spells wore off for this last leg. Domitia and Razan would have to sneak through on foot and utterly exposed.

"C'mon. I saw a ship in port with Fellmire flags. Could be a refugee ship. We've at least got to warn them."

Domitia dragged Razan around a corner into an alley... and directly into a pair with a great shield and a mage's stave. Razan stumbled to the floor, tripping over his own feet.

"Whoa, there!" said a deep-throated, guttural voice.

"Pop and maw-maw!?" He looked up and squinted.

Grandma Lise had her old college mage's stave, a sixty-year-old relic at this point. But it could still sling spells. Grandpa Nasir had a shield and a spear in each hand.

"Pumpkin?" Lise breathed deeply, relieved. "Well, we arrived back in town to find everything on fire. Not sure what everyone's after, but we're here to make sure the family is okay."

"There was an angry mob at the keep!" Razan said, rising to his feet. "We're trying to get out of town. There's a ship in port..."

Nasir nodded. "Right. We'll cover your flank. Just like the ol' crusade maneuvers."

"Oh, dear, that was a lifetime ago," said Lise. "Your hip isn't anywhere near as strong as it was back then. Just let my spells do the talking."

"Go," Grandpa Nasir urged the pair.

"Indeed." Lise nodded. "Nobody is going after our gobdaughter-in-law."

"You're... not supposed to use the g-word like that anymore, maw-maw," said Razan.

"Oh, well, you know." Grandma Lise looked around bashfully. "Just be sure to write, sweetums."

Gramps and Grandma held down the alleyway, misdirecting any angry mobs that stopped by and otherwise blocking their grandson's path as he and Domitia ran for the docks.

13

The docks were quiet enough, the late unpleasantness having scared away commerce. Certainly, most ships had chosen to anchor away from the port with torch-wielding mobs loose. Only a single ship remained, with a gangplank waiting to cast off at any time.

Razan helped Domitia balance on the way up. They emerged onto a deck full of gob-kin. Some still wore their heavy Shiverfast cloaks, while others Razan even recognized from downtown Rivergale.

"Dom? Domitia? Everyone, lay off. They're one of ours!" A tall-ish gob-kin dressed like a pirate emerged from the captain's quarters.

"Normlok!" Domitia said. "Don't worry, Razan's with me. This is that nice human boy I've told you about."

Another four burly brothers stood up.

"You all made it." Domitia's face lit up. "Even Grob!"

That first pirate-looking fellow, Normlok, limped over.

"Fleshy human, eh?" He eyed Razan up and down, teeth bared.

Duly, Razan noted that this was his first meeting with an of-age brother of Domitia's.

"He's…" Domitia rested her hands at her midsection and glanced away. "He's already fathered a litter."

The gob-man's eyes widened. He looked at Domitia's waist as if confirming the sight. Then back to Razan, then back to Domitia. It was a maneuver echoed by the other brothers.

"So, you... you don't need to do any crossbow-polishing intimidation tactics. It's a little late." Domitia nodded. "Look, it's already done. His toe dipped in the ol' ritual pool last summer without realizing it, we think. So, I'd better not hear any growling about upholding my honor or anything, because if so I'll-"

But Norm grabbed Razan in a bear hug and twirled him around. A great cry came from the ship captain's mandibles.

"Brother!!!"

The other brothers echoed the shout.

Norm boisterously placed Razan back on the deck a, facing the gob-kin crowd.

"This human is part of the clan," said Norm.

The other brothers roared their approval.

The ship steamed along the southern coast for Fellmire, captained by Domitia's brother, Normlok. This shore was winding, increasing the travel time by many days. All the while, Razan and Domitia huddled amongst refugees in conditions so crowded they scarcely had room for a cot. Domitia's brothers helped the pair with rations and the like.

By the time they finally reached Fellmire again, few came up on the top deck to watch the ship pull into port. Everyone was too exhausted. Half of Fellmire was at the docks waiting for them.

Despite the crowds and despite everyone climbing out of the boat all at once, Domitia's mother and aunt still found them.

Most of the brothers hadn't seen the rest of the family in years. Indeed, Domitia was the only one who'd seen their youngest half-siblings.

They'd likely be safe from any anti-gob mob here in Fellmire. Razan sighed, about the only human on the dock. But the burrow came and embraced him all the same. It would be tough going for a time, and it was still up in the air if he'd ever see the old ancestral family keep again. But here Razan was, with the in-laws for the near future.

14

"Hard to believe it's been so many years already."

Razan had grown a fair bit older. Grew a slight beard since graduating from mage's college. He had to look the part!

"Well, here we are again," he continued. "Another Wintersgrip festival. Another visit to the grandparents."

Domitia was there, looking a bit more like her mother each day. She held onto Razan's hand, twin marriage bands on their ring fingers –alexandrite-inlaid Fellmire gob-iron for the husband, and Rivergale emerald amidst a gold-hued band for the missus.

The pair stood at the edge of a glen amidst the Rivergale forests. Short grass cropped up in and around local mausoleums of big-name landholding families.

"They were always very nice to me," Domitia said, gently rubbing her husband's hand with her thumb.

"You must have made quite the first impression." Razan chuckled. "Grandpa always did enjoy jousting. I'm sure that helped thaw things out."

Domitia smiled, recalling a long and storied semi-professional jousting career. She'd won three more tourneys at a Fellmire postgrad institution, and even a few in the Fellmire minor leagues.

"So, here we are," the red-headed gob-kin said.

"Indeed." Razan knelt. "Hey, Grandpa Nasir, Grandma Lise. We were off to Fellmire for a while after college. We couldn't make it for a few Wintersgrip festivals. And before you know it, we had new responsibilities to take care of."

The pair knelt before a pair of simple headstones. Nasir and Grandma Lise passed away within a year or so of each other, about five years prior. And at Domitia and Razan's feet were not one, not five, but nine squirming and inattentive gob-human hybrids, too young to truly grasp the significance of the tombstones.

Gregnarb, Nasirgrok, and Amanda took after their father's side of the family a great deal. They had Razan's nose, especially Greg,' with the addition of a mild green complexion.

Lisa and Rutitia, meanwhile, could have passed for clones of their mother. They tended to bite their father's ankles.

And Gerald, Bianka, Cassandra, and Yorblarg all took a bit from mom, a bit from dad. Yorblarg had Grandpa Nasir's features, while Cass had a bit of Lise.

"Now, now, children. These are the graves of your great-grandparents," Domitia said.

"Yorblarg ate my dire-chicken!" Nasirgrok whined. "And I was saving it for a special occasion."

Razan cleared his throat sharply. "Children. Children! Gobnorgernackep blesses those who respect their departed elders."

That got half the children listening. Domitia smiled warmly; her darling husband had adopted the faith of gob-kind more devoutly than she ever did. Still, it was nice that he was so interested in her family's culture.

They'd lived the past half-decade in Fellmire. And so, Razan's poor grandparents had never seen their great-grandkids before they passed.

"Daddy, are these your great-grand-grans, or mommy's?" Asked Rutitia, her adult tusks just barely growing in.

"They were mine, dear. Mom's family all lives back home in Fellmire. You've met them."

"Did they ever meet mommy?" Rutitia asked again.

"Well." Razan and Domitia looked at each other. "That's quite the long story."

"And wouldn't you know it, it involves jousting," Domitia said.

"So, get situated, children, this will take a while..."

ACKNOWLEDGEMENT

A special thanks to Ari for creating my cover. Go visit her via Bluesky or wherever fine social media is sold @arianwen44.

ABOUT THE AUTHOR

Adam K. Armbrust

The mysterious pen name of a novice author. Not a sentient AI granted flesh and let loose upon the publishing world. Currently exploring ways to Kindle-ify a modest backlog of other short stories. Stay tuned.

A modest list of available stories can be seen here: akarmbrustauthor.wordpress.com

Also working ono a LitRPG, which you may find via RoyalRoad under this same name. It will eventually reach Kindle and hopefully audiobook in three volumes, just as soon as I work out how to make tables remotely viable or otherwise convert them to something more legible.

www.ingramcontent.com/pod-product-compliance
Lightning Source LLC
Chambersburg PA
CBHW020546130626
46552CB00007B/2768